Ann Boone

For Elizabeth, who read it

The man stood beside his vehicle, because he was sick of sitting in it. He pulled another cigarette out of the pack. What did this make, seven, ten, who was counting? How long had he been waiting? He was tired of waiting, but he had orders to follow. Suddenly, two specks of light came bouncing in the distance. Headlights. Finally.

Chapter 1

Sometimes ordinary things take on a whole new meaning. A stop light catches you, and prevents you from being involved in an accident. A front porch light is left on in the daytime, and you find out the inhabitants never made it home. Ordinary things become extraordinary when later events are examined in light of them.

For me, the ordinary thing was a parked van that led me to a murder, then another, nearly being killed myself, and finding drug traffic in the underbelly of our small town.

It all started when my daughter Elizabeth said, "Hasn't that van been there for a while," as we were preparing for "take-off" onto the interstate near our home.

Most people think you drive on interstates, but on ours, we fly. You press the gas pedal as hard as you can and barrel out into the line of traffic with a copy of your updated will in hand. If you are in a little car like I am, the big truckers play "smash 'em" with your bumper. I drive really fast.

It is a dangerous entrance ramp. My first thought was that the driver of the pine green Aerostar had pulled off to catch his breath. Long breath. Elizabeth was right; I had seen that van for three days.

"I'll call Billy," I said, referring to our local sheriff.

He's a friend of mine since I got to know him as a newspaper reporter in our town covering local politics. I have a lot of respect for my friend.

Since Billy got elected, he has set out to end corruption in the sheriff's department, putting a stop to "lunches" across the county line at the Red Carpet Inn. Those lunch morsels turned out to be the kind with platinum highlights in their hair. That put a bad taste in some of his deputies' mouths, and they like to take it out on me since they see my support of him as being one of the reasons he got elected.

It's true I did stories on him, but it is also true I did it because he was newsworthy in cleaning up our county of corruption. Billy won his election because the people of this county wanted him to, but that does not stop the deputies who don't like him from mistreating me.

I had to drop Elizabeth off at high school for a school newspaper meeting, (gee, I wonder where she gets that) at 7:00 A.M., so it was too early to try the sheriff's office business line, and I didn't want to bother Central Dispatch with such a trivial matter. I'd call Billy later after I'd been at the office awhile.

Every time I dial the sheriff's department number, I am

saying the rosary, (and I'm not even Roman Catholic), that Bruce "The Bull" Tyner, one of the deputies who hates Billy, will not pick it up. He's the worst of the bunch: snide, uneducated and boorish. Dealing with him is like fighting a storm. It can be dangerous if you are not on your guard, and there is simply no reasoning with it ...or him. If he has the opportunity to make my life more difficult, he will.

His hatred for me is more personal than me just helping Billy in his quest. I caught Bruce in flagrante delicto once, down a dirt road near my house when I was out walking my dogs. He could not possibly have been interrogating that girl in the back seat. I reported his activity to the old sheriff, too naïve to know that when something wasn't done, it was because the sheriff was doing the same thing. Bruce still has his job because the evidence I had given the old sheriff miraculously disappeared, and the reprobate had the sense not to let me catch him at it again.

If I were a buxom blonde, Bruce would have his tongue hanging out, stumbling all over himself to do my bidding. If I were a big girl, I could beat him up, but I am just a scrawny brunette with hope in my heart that people will do the right thing.

Billy has offered to give me his private number, but I think that would just inspire rumors about our relationship, and in a small town that is worse than death. We've only known each other for four years, since he ran for election and I covered his campaign. I'd known him from reputation before that, but as I got to know him personally, he was exactly as he appeared, and that is a rare thing.

Billy is happily married, so private phone calls from single women just ask for trouble, even though Billy's wife, Melba, wouldn't mind if I did call, because Melba is my friend, too.

Melba and Billy grew up in this small town, Morton, and got married as everyone expected them to. They dated in high school. He played football; she was the senior class secretary. She went to the local college and got her Associates degree to become a medical transcriptionist; he went to become a law enforcement officer. Their life together may appear mundane to some, but it is sound and peaceful, and gives people something to hope for in this world where marriage seems to have lost its solid standing.

I met them both during the campaign, a time for stress and falseness. For many politicians, a wife can make or break a political career. But Billy wasn't trying to establish a political career; he was trying to clean up this county. That's what first struck me about him. He was so honest and pure, he reminded me of an innocent child in the woods. He is anything but, reminding me now of Teddy Roosevelt and his "Walk softly and carry a big stick" image.

Melba was calm and sure of herself. She didn't resort to patronizing techniques to support her husband. Our friendship is based on this solid ground. We have always been forthright with each other. Melba knows I'm not after her husband, something widows get accused of, even if it is just the wife's insecurity talking.

Watch how women behave towards a recently divorced or widowed woman. Women who were your friends are now afraid of you. Men you trusted try to wrestle you to the ground at the first sign of an opening. Maybe all you did was say, "Hello," or give them a welcome hug. This is interpreted as "Gosh, I miss my husband, and I need a man."

I don't tell people the story of how my husband died. People think it is because it is too painful to talk about, and I cultivate that idea. The real reason I don't talk about it is because I always burst out laughing, not an appropriate response when you talk about a tragedy.

The problem is that this image appears in my mind: my husband with his hands on his hips, that smirk on his face, his testy voice telling me I didn't know what I was talking about, that the beam he had just put up in our house was as solid as a ...That's it. I don't know what the beam was as solid as because he never finished the simile. After I recovered from the shock, this comical image is all that remains. I guess that doesn't say much for my marriage.

The children were young, so it has seemed normal for it to be just us ever since.

I moved to Morton from my own small town, nearby, for a fresh start: new home, new career, new people. Only, they, the people, seemed oddly the same. I guess wherever you go in Small Town, America you find that to be true. You have heroes and villains, the good, the bad and the ugly.

I glanced in my rear view mirror to see a police cruiser slide out of the trees and into the lane behind me. Most people react to police cars following them with an elevated heart rate, sweaty palms and dry mouth. Emily Dickinson said she always felt "zero at the bone" when she saw "the narrow fellow in the grass"- a snake. When I see a city police cruiser following me through town, I feel like I've just stumbled across a snake unexpectedly. My reaction is the same.

I should be used to it by now, since the city officers follow me any time they see me out to intimidate me. They are Billy's enemies, so they are mine.

Sometimes, just to spite them, I exaggerate my attention to the traffic laws. I stop for an inordinately long time at stop signs; I never slide through yellow lights, but slow almost to a stop when I see them. I go, not just the speed limit, but two miles under it. It's a wonder I ever make it to work on time. Oh, wait, I make it up when I speed at 110 mph on the interstate.

Chapter 2

"Shurff's Offs," a snapping, growling voice bellowed across the sheriff's office phone lines when I got around to making the call that morning. Just my luck, it was my nemesis, Bruce Tyner.

"This is Mibbie Wright, may I speak to Sheriff Bartlett?" I said, knowing exactly what was coming next.

"Well, I don't know. *Can you?*"

This was Tyner's way of taunting me. He is a country boy who picked up quickly that I try to use good grammar because I used to be an English teacher. He sees it as being condescending. I've tried to mend my ways and use slang, bad grammar, and other foul-tasting forms of speech, but my innate sense of articulation just takes over. God love him, he thinks you are SUPPOSED to say, "can." I didn't bite.

"Yes, may," I repeated.

"Well, he ain't in," Tyner said, or I should say, barked.

I knew better than to leave a message. It wouldn't get to Billy anyway.

"Thanks," I said and hung up. I learned a long time ago not to prolong pain. End it just as soon as you can.

I got busy with my calendar. It was a big desk-size thing with my interview schedule scrawled in at hourly intervals.

Even though you don't get paid for 60-hour-work weeks, as a reporter, you still put those kinds of hours in. The best way to deal with that is to coordinate as many interviews or photo ops as possible. I had an interview with the new principal at the high school, another interview with an exchange student and a city council prep meeting for tomorrow night's regular session.

The town has grown enough that the city council couldn't just show up for a vote anymore. They had to actually know what they were talking about.

I could cover all that in two hours if I got the exchange student to meet me in the Morton High School lobby, and that would give Billy enough time to get into the office. Maybe I would just stop by. My ear was still burning from Tyner's dragon voice, and my friend Gayle worked the front desk. She'd let me in to see Billy.

I sipped some water to quiet a cough that seemed to be creeping on. I'd stopped in for a quick check at the doctor's office out of deference to my children. I didn't stay around to hear the results out of deference to me. I don't like doctors.

The new principal seemed like a good choice, and after my interview with him, I had a few minutes to review my questions for the exchange student I was meeting.

She was punctual to our interview, a quality I like in young people. She was from the Netherlands and spoke English fluently. She was a little large, blonde, with an average face and piercing Norwegian blue eyes. All of these were good physical qualities because she wouldn't be prey to the confident, self-assured boys at the local high school, or the brunt of jealousy from the "beautiful" girls.

I wondered about her host family, though. The mom was a harried mother of four, and had insisted on this interview as well as being present and bringing her kids along. The mother wanted all her friends to know she was hosting an exchange student, a fact she kept referring to as her "overseas experience."

Bretta, the exchange student, was constantly being interrupted from our interview by the mom handing her the youngest child, a baby of one, to tend. The mom even wanted me to take a picture with her, the kids and Bretta, even though the story was supposed to be just about Bretta.

I am always ready for this. I pretend to take a wide-angle shot, but, really, I focus in tight on my chosen subject. If the mom calls to complain about the fact that she and the kids aren't in the photo, I will simply tell her I had to resize it for the page, and the original didn't fit. I don't like being manipulated.

I was worried about Bretta. A little known fact, and dark secret of the exchange program is that if you are not careful, it starts to look like white slavery. The mom was one of those whiney types that you wanted to shake. She said, "Stop," to her kids the way most drunks say "more" to the bartender. Her kids were hoodlums who ran all over the high school lobby even as small as it was.

I don't appreciate mothers who don't discipline their children. Nobody likes a little brat; they grow up to be big brats. Besides, if parents really thought about it, they would like to live with well-disciplined children themselves. Too

10

often, these lazy parents foist their spoiled children off on an unsuspecting public. The public, in turn, is left to clean up the mess these parents could have avoided with a little effort early on.

Bretta was pleasant enough in the situation, but she'd only arrived in America a week ago. I would need to keep an eye on this young girl. I can't help myself. I was the same way as a teacher. I could see the kids who were hiding things and needed an advocate. Bretta seemed to be more of a nanny than a visiting exchange student.

The city council session was a gift. Billy had to be there because of some zoning issues. The city police hated the county police ever since Billy came along. With Billy's guys actually doing some law enforcement in their district, the city police were being shown up for not doing it in theirs.

Now, like the proverbial dog in Aesop's manger, they wanted turf wars over jurisdiction. They didn't want to "police" their own zones, but they sure weren't going to let Billy's boys get credit for doing it. I set up my tape recorder and took out my notepad.

Billy smiled at me, and I mouthed, "Need a minute." He nodded in response. Good. We could talk in the council boardroom, all the better to stop wagging tongues. The usual griping and complaining about having to meet finally gave way to actual business.

The mayor is one of those young guys who finally broke the "Good Old Boy" template of being the oldest guy on the council to run and be elected. It was tradition, in this little town, that the most experienced council member took the reins of power, and that usually meant at age 84. Progress was not this little town's forte.

Garth Miller was from the community born and bred, and came to the council seat at age 32 because his daddy passed on. Maybe the voters counted that as experience, and that was why he was the sitting mayor at the very young age of 45. They say his mama guarded his marital status, culling out most of his marital prospects, but I had seen him in the big city near us being cozy with someone of the same gender, so I suspected his mama's interference was to his liking.

Garth was a progressive thinker, which the town needed. He was also about an "8.2" on the male pride Richter scale which the town didn't need. I had also seen him with some pretty shady business characters. He had acted alarmed when our eyes met, then sullen and furtive. I might have ignored it, but my "Something's Up" radar blipped violently.

We had all kinds of shady characters in our town, like the car dealer who had a gambling casino in the dealership garage, the appliance guy who was running moonshine in his appliance van, and the pharmacist who was selling drugs on the side. You couldn't sit down at our local restaurant without sitting next to a shady character, but these were *our* shady characters and we knew how to keep them under control.

Garth seemed to have some new shady characters we didn't know. I think he suspected my quiet knowledge, but he usually treated me with the right measure of indifference and respect.

After the meeting, Billy sat still. I joined him.

"What do you know about a dark green Aerostar on my exit ramp?"

I could say it like that because Billy knew his county inside and out. Even though it was the largest county in the state of Alabama, and they didn't give him enough manpower to run it, he tended the county like I had tended my classroom. I knew every nook and cranny; so did he.

"It's been there a couple of days hasn't it?" he asked, his brow crinkling in thought. "Any decals?"

He was speaking of the orange stickers the state police put on the window of abandoned vehicles. This helps them keep up with how long vehicles have been stranded and whether or not they should be towed.

"None that I saw," I said, "but then, I didn't examine it. Think it'd be okay?"

"Examine it? You thinking of becoming one of my detectives?" he smiled.

"No, I'm just trying to save my hard-working sheriff some time by checking on this for him. With so few guys working for you, are you going to turn down some free help? Strictly off the payroll," I smiled one of my angelic, beatific, "aren't-I-sweeter-than-two-spoonfuls-of-sugar" smiles.

"What makes you suspicious?"

"Out-of-state plates; been there a while; next to the mountain; woman's intuition."

That last one made *him* smile. It was the reason I gave for most of the things I did that seemed out of the ordinary. Women's intuition, don't under-estimate it.

"Didn't examine it, huh?"

I hated to admit that I had driven back to look it over after dropping Elizabeth off at the high school. "Well, my powers of observation just took over. I mean, I didn't get out to take a *really* good look."

Actually, I have a lousy sense of observation. Once, a professor tested his theory that we don't really look at the world around us, even when it conks us on the head. He had a guy come into our classroom and make a big scene about finding a place on campus. Then the guy just stormed out. Later, the professor asked us what we saw. Only a handful of us actually saw him. Most of us were paying attention to each other, or the notes from the previous day.

I saw the guy, but when it comes to physical descriptions, I can't give you one. I am envious of the people who can say, "Average height 6 '1", weight, 208, medium build, sandy blonde hair, blue eyes." If it didn't sound so ethereal, I'd describe suspects like this: "He had an aura of wickedness about him. His eyes bored into you like he meant to do you harm." That doesn't work for police composites.

Economy won out, and rather than sending a paid officer, Billy agreed I should check out the van and see if there was any need to pursue it. As we exited the council boardroom, we nearly bumped into Garth Miller. That was strange. I could not imagine why he had been there. If he had forgotten something from his briefcase, why didn't he just come inside and get it? If he needed Billy, why didn't he talk to him now?

As it was, it looked like he had been watching Billy and me in conversation, trying to find out what we were talking about. His look gave me a shiver. Billy spoke to him, but Garth didn't answer. He just turned on his heel and stalked away from us.

I went back to the office to check my calendar for the next appointments, arrange for lunch and type my three new stories. Our secretary is a modern version of Selma Diamond, a character from *Night Court,* a sit-com from the 80's. She has a gravelly voice and is all of four feet tall. You expect her to have a cigarette hanging out of her mouth, but it will be a pencil that she has used to take illegible messages for you.

Since I was going to have to consult an Egyptologist as to who had called and why, because Gladys's handwriting would pass for hieroglyphics, I typed up the wedding announcements, births and the obituaries. We put them on the same page so people will get the good news and the bad news at the same time.

Chapter 3

Too late in the day for what I deem reasonable working hours, I was headed home, and the van was there. I made a turn up the entrance ramp and stopped right behind it. This time, I didn't hesitate to make a thorough inspection: older model van, maybe an '88. I'd had one. No apparent damage like water or antifreeze on the ground from a water pump, to make it stop, but ask the girl who has had three transmissions, and I'll tell you there is no visible evidence *it's* gone out. However, the car won't get you far when they go.

So, maybe the problem was the transmission. No baby seats inside the passenger area. No "woman's junk", or man's either, but there was evidence of a meal.

Hardee's wrappers and an old drink cup were in the center between the seats. There's a Hardee's two exits back, and it looked like the driver may have stopped there, then stopped here to eat, but, why here? This is a lonely stretch of road, even with the busy interstate above.

This side of the interstate looks like the roadsides in the mountainous regions of North Carolina, stretching up almost immediately from the roadside into a forested-tipped cliff. It's beautiful, but deserted, and not necessarily a safe place to stop for a meal. There are no lights here at night. Even the oncoming headlights from traffic on the interstate above don't shine down here.

Outside the van, there were cigarette butts. Not the kind that someone emptied out of an ashtray, but several, like someone had taken the time to smoke while he sat for a while, in one place. I got my camera out of my car and shot some pictures, the journalist in me taking over. Still no stickers from the state troopers, so I took down the tag number and dialed the sheriff's department.

"Please, please, please," I whimpered, begging God to have mercy on me and not make me talk to Bruce again.

"Marshall County Sheriff's Department," Gayle's voice rang out melodiously.

"Thank God," I said. Oops, did I say that out loud?

"I beg your pardon."

"Sorry Gayle, I'm just so glad to hear your voice."

"Yes?" Gayle said back, in no hurry to make friends on the phone.

If you don't know her, you may think she is abrupt. In reality, she is a professional in a world gone mad. She knows her job and she does it thoroughly. She doesn't put up with people who try to get special treatment from the sheriff's office, but she would never be rude. She will tell you what you need to know, but she won't let you push her around to get more.

I like Gayle. She wants people to play by the rules. The first time I met her was right after Billy took office. She was already putting up the metaphorical walls then, not letting people talk to him when all they wanted was to waste the time of "the next man in power." I thought hiring Gayle was one of the smartest things Billy did. I respected her immediately, even if she did seem a bit prickly.

"Gayle, it's me, Mibbie, is Billy in?"

"Oh, why didn't you say so? I know your mama taught you better phone manners than to just start talking."

"She did. I'm sorry. I told Billy I would check out a strange car and I have the tag number. Do you want to take it down, or should I tell him?"

I always do this for Gayle. She is a very busy woman. I try to help her out with passing on information. She trusts me not to waste the taxpayer's money with Billy by staying on the phone with nonsense, so she usually patches me through.

"Hold on, I think he's free."

I hummed along to the instrumental version of "Rescue Me." I know not to sing. Anyone who heard me would have me arrested for disturbing the peace. I have absolutely no ability when it comes to singing, but just to spite the world, when I am alone, I sing really loud.

Such was not the case, now, because at any moment Gayle would come back on the line. If she heard me, she might refuse to ever let me call again. I think it is important to recognize your weaknesses.

"Hey kid, what's up?"

I like that about Billy. I'm pushing 45 and he still calls me "kid."

"Here's the tag number." I read it off. "It looks like it may have been a rendezvous. I don't think there was any car trouble. Who can handle this, you guys, or the state troopers?

Do we know anybody over there now?"

Getting cooperation is no different in any business, including police work. What matters is "who" you know.

"Yeah, I think I have one friend left in the trooper office; it will be theirs," Billy laughed.

Billy's election had been hard won, and the guys on the other side of the fence, whether they were in the sheriff's department, the city police department, or the state trooper's office, were not happy to have someone like Billy with his moral standards in office. Just like kids, they wanted someone with no morals, or at least theirs. It's a shame the people of this county almost chose to stay with a crooked sheriff. I like to think they just didn't know.

I got off the phone quickly. I knew Gayle would be watching the red light on the switchboard to see when it stopped blinking and to see if her faith in me was well founded by not keeping the phone tied up too long. Afterward, I backed down the interstate. While this is a dangerous and illegal procedure, it would be far more dangerous for me to have tried to enter the interstate's whizzing traffic line and return to my exit by the correct method.

I meandered home for dinner. My children are in various stages of young adulthood, one in college and two in high school. One of the nicest things they did was take over cooking dinner when my job keeps me out late. The welcome smell of rich Tuscan olive oil and tangy tomato sauce let me know we were in for spaghetti. Elizabeth grinned from the stove.

19

"Almost ready; have a good day?"

"Yes, and your query is almost answered," I said.

"Which one was that? New cell phone or a later curfew?"

"No such luck," I smiled. Kids never stop trying. "The one about that van on the interstate."

"What'd you find out?"

"Nothing yet, Billy's going to let me know who can check it out."

We piled our plates high with steaming pasta and warm, crusty French bread, and went into the den to watch a movie. We're cheap dates, all of us. Good food, a good movie and we're set for life.

Chapter 4

I do this most mornings. I wake up too early and look out the window.

"Is it a reasonable hour for a sane person to be awake?" I ask myself before finally giving in and getting up.

Like most people, I learned the hard way that one of the most precious things in the world is a good night's sleep. Ask anyone who has been denied it by pain, materially or emotionally, and they will tell you in no uncertain terms, sleep is the most precious thing.

Insomniacs are quite aware of how unnatural their night habitation is, so they usually don't say anything about it. I try not to number myself among them. But, give me a worry, a trying time, and that is where it will get me: sleepless.

It hadn't helped that I had been kept awake all night by the sound of four-wheelers going up and down the power lines near my house. They were far enough away that when I finally roused from sleep, I could not really hear them, but the noise invaded my subconscious and would not permit real sleep to come.

The next thing I began doing was a mental calculation of all the things I can do in such and such amount of time. That's why if I wake up early, I am sure to be late for work. I'll spend all my "extra" time doing things that have to be done and run out of the time I thought I had. After laying in the bed making up my daily "To Do" list, I looked out the window.

The sun was a little orange ball, so I judged it to be about 6:30, and the clock reinforced that belief, a decent enough hour to be up and stirring. I always look at my behavior as if I'm on a reality show. Of course, if I were on a reality show, nothing would be further from the truth. I would manipulate and finagle my way through the whole thing to make myself look nicer, more competent, and fresh as a daisy. That is not reality.

Today's list consisted of figuring out why I couldn't get that parked van out of my head, and I was anxious to get started. If it was going to be the nag that kept me awake, the sooner I dispensed with it the better my dream life was going to be.

One of the magical things about waking up early is being alone, feeling the whole new day is just yours and that everything, including the sunrise, the cool breath of morning air and the song of the birds belongs to you. But, the cardinal rule of early risers is not to think the world is awake with you. Don't pick up the phone thinking everyone else had a long list of things to do, too. I have lost more friends that way.

So, if I couldn't call anybody, I could make a list of people I *could* call at 8:00 A.M.

First: Billy, so I could find out which one of our State Trooper friends had a lead on the car.

Second: the so-named State Trooper.

If I were more tech savvy, I could hack into the

Department of Motor Vehicles, or as it is known in the modern vernacular, the DMV, but I am incompetent when it comes to technology besides being the world's worst criminal.

I couldn't even get into mischief when I was young. None of my friends wanted me along for high school pranks because I am the kid that got caught when we were just in the planning stages. We didn't even have to buy the shaving cream and toilet paper for me to be hauled into the principal's office.

Early on, my co-conspirators used me as a decoy. They planted worthless information in me and committed their criminal acts while I was incarcerated in the bad-student cubby. Nope, everything I did had to be on the up-and-up, or I'd surely get caught.

This however, is not how my heroes like Dashiel Hammett's famous hard-boiled detective Sam Spade operated. Sam walked the thin line of right and wrong to get the criminal off the street. Since I did not have his skill, I was going to have to walk the whole four-lane interstate of right, instead of the balance beam middle of maybe right.

I showered and dressed for work, sipping coffee as I made lunches for my girls. Teenagers typically avoid breakfast, but I am a firm believer in starting the morning right, so I whipped up some scrambled eggs with rich, sharp cheddar cheese. I snuggled them in between two slices of French bread lightly toasted with butter and slipped them into plastic bags. The girls would be in a hurry and needed to grab and go.

Later, at the office, my calendar indicated I already had three interviews set up. One of them was at the courthouse as a follow-up story on an embezzlement scheme. I'd done the initial story about three weeks ago. I had a lot of sympathy for this guy. He was just a small town kid who got put in charge of the bank's finances because he was the bank president's daughter's brother-in-law. Suddenly he has all this money and he forgets that it isn't his. It crosses his desk everyday, so why not?

Bless his heart. The poor guy had looked baffled when the judge read the charges to him. His attorney, who was the bank president's wife's cousin, stated emphatically, "Not guilty, your honor," and poor, embezzling Roger just looked pitifully at both of them like some puppy who had gotten caught in the middle of making a mess, and wasn't sure what to do next. I felt sorry for him, because I could see myself doing something like that and not realizing the implications. I didn't approve of him taking the money; I just saw how the line got blurred for a guy who knew so little about his job.

The court case I would be covering today was his sentencing. While I was at the courthouse, I could easily slip into the DMV office and have a word with the State Trooper Billy would name. Things were coming together.

I should never think, or worse, say that. The evidence of that was in the phone call I made next.

"Shurff's Offs," my worst nightmare growled into the phone when I dialed Billy. Uh-Oh, did I say, "Coming together?" Yes, I had. Now I paid.

I thought I had waited long enough for Gayle to show

up. I had dawdled over coffee, even taken time to make breakfast. I had driven only 120 MPH on the interstate to get to work, not the usual 150. I had sat at my computer and typed the preliminary passages of my bank story. I had paid the "waste as much time as you can, while still doing something worthwhile" dues. Apparently, not enough.

"May I speak to Gayle?" I asked, knowing Bruce was going to know who it was. After all, I am the only person he knows who uses the proper form to ask for her and doesn't ask for her like this: "Gayle'n?"

"Well, I don't know, can you?" Here we go again.

"Right," I said, willing him to have his fun, just get me through to Gayle.

"Nope." Nothing more. I was going to have to beat it out of him. And believe me if I could have traded in my 5' 1" frame for a 6'2" one, I would have.

"When will she be in?"

"I dunno." Okay, my turn.

"Thanks," and I hung up. No point in prolonging the misery.

Somewhere in heaven, God smiled at me, and my strength of character in not giving into my barbaric tendencies to beat the uncooperative senseless. The phone rang, and it was Billy.

"Hey, kid," he said after listening to my: "*The World.* May I help you?"

Now, why we called our newspaper *The World* when we only cover county news is beyond me. But here, things continue as tradition whether they make sense or not. It's

25

tradition, after all, and small towns thrive on that.

"I am so glad to hear your voice." I practically yelled at him. That lack of sleep thing may actually be a problem.

"Okay," Billy said laughing. "I hope you're still this happy after I tell you what we've got. The van is out-of-state like you thought. Marvin Treadwell is our connection at the Trooper's office. He said they didn't have a record of it. He took your numbers and ran the plates. You won't be surprised to hear this, but it was reported stolen last week. Somebody heisted it from Atlanta, the car stealing capital of the nation. You remember you did a story on stolen cars showing that criminals were more likely to steal Ford Escorts than they were Jaguars?

"Well, this is one of those situations. A Ford van melts into the traffic. It doesn't catch the attention of the police as easily. The person who owns it wants it back more than the police want to keep it, but can't pay the towing fee to get it back, so it gets lost in the shuffle. Limited resources kind of thing. Marvin says they'll haul it in for forensics to have a look, but it's more likely a case of joy riding gone bad. Can I do anything else to help?"

He is such a sweetie!

"No thanks," I said. "I'll take it up with Marvin. Am I going to stir up trouble if I talk to him?"

I always ask this. The lines are clearly drawn in this town as if we all wore matching jerseys to show our support of which team we were on. The bad guys are just biding their time until the election this November so they can get rid of Billy. They are also tallying up his friends. If he loses, there will be retribution of the most unpleasant kind.

This means that only the most fearless, honest law enforcement agents are on Billy's side. I would trust them with my children's lives and that is saying a lot. After all, what does my own life mean without my children? If I say I trust them with my life, well, that is just a worthless statement, but trusting them with my children, says a lot.

So, I try to protect Billy's friends as much as possible. Sometimes that includes not acknowledging them in public or talking to them in front of other people.

"Don't worry," Billy said. "Marvin is lead."

This was a local colloquialism that meant Marvin was close enough to pension that they couldn't hurt him and far enough from the fray that the bad guys couldn't make his life miserable. Seniority has its privileges.

I thanked Billy and made a note to stop by to see Officer Treadwell at 9:30 A.M. The bank case was high on the docket, so I should be out in a jiffy. No matter who the embezzler was kin to, he would get a fair trial.

It was a good thing we could boast honest judges in this county for whatever else our law enforcement agents resembled. I guess it was because they all came from old money. You simply can't bribe a judge who already has more money than the Federal Reserve.

Of course the judges could have been blackmailed by skeletons, but our judge's wives had dug very deep graves and swept them all in. Some people may say that is wrong. I say as long as the guys are doing the right thing now, let their pasts go. Besides, the judges had been candid enough with me about their errant ways. They had been young, made their mistakes, moved on. Now they were a set of the most righteous set of judges I had seen since the Old Testament. It was a pleasure to watch them in action.

I shoved a piece of bread in the toaster oven in our makeshift kitchen at the office. There is nothing more embarrassing than having your stomach growl in the solemn quiet of courtroom proceedings. It can also be quite unnerving to the person on trial. I remembered too late why we have a sign above the oven saying "Don't butter your bread before you put it in to toast" when Steve yelled, "Mibbie, the oven's on fire again!"

Drat, won't I ever learn? And they always know it's me.

Chapter 5

Marvin Treadwell was the picture of strength even with his age on the other side of 50. He towered, not only in stature, but also in moral character. You could feel it. He wore it like skin, not just a badge as some people have.

The "badge sort" put on morality for convenience, but took it off just as easily. He was a cross between the honest good looks of John Wayne and the sly all-knowing coolness of Robert Mitchum. I was in love.

Marvin is safe like Billy, happily married to a great woman. She was the kind of woman who expected you to be in love with her husband, but you'd better keep your passions under control because you could also expect her to protect her turf. Besides, any untoward female attention was met with Marvin's own stalwart aloofness. No silly schoolboy behavior from this one.

And like Billy, he couldn't help teasing me.

"So Billy's got himself a new detective. Mibbie, are things that tough in the newspaper business that now you've got to moonlight?" he grinned that big irresistible grin. I picked myself up off the floor.

"Stop confusing me with your devastating charm. What about that van? I'm losing sleep over it." I coughed a little.

"Whoa girl! We've got it over at forensics, but it takes time. You the owner or something because I have never, and

I mean never, seen someone so worked up over an old Ford Aerostar before. I'd hate to see what happens to you when you go to a car auction."

I had to laugh. It did look like an overreaction didn't it?

"Okay, do you have anything more than what you told Billy?"

"Uh-Uh," Marvin said, "but as soon as the report is in, I'll give you a ring."

"Good enough." And I patted Marvin on the arm on the way out.

Garth Miller, the mayor, was in the hall. Not just in the hall, but near the door, like he had been at the council room the day before, as though he were listening in on my conversation with Marvin. I nearly mowed him down as I came out. Had he been trying to listen in again? How did he know I was there? Was it my imagination when a chill ran down my spine? No, not the "Gosh-he-is-so-good-looking" kind of chill, but the "Oh No! Is-that-Satan's-spawn?" kind of chill. Combined with the council meeting episode, this seemingly non-coincidental second meeting scared me.

Garth was watching me; his eyes followed me right out the door. If I'd been Sam Spade, I would have wheeled around, marched right up to his so-cute-you-could-pinch-him face and demand to know what he wanted, or at least made some clever, smart aleck comment like this:

"So Garth, did they finally shut down your massage parlor?"

"Hey, Garth. I didn't expect to see you until I actually preferred charges against you."

Even the tired old "Take a picture it'll last longer" phrase would have been better than what I did.

I slunk out the door like I had done something to feel guilty about. Not one clever remark in me. Gosh, I hate myself sometimes.

Chapter 6

Okay, I don't believe in coincidences. I may as well just admit it. I was going to sit there at my desk at the newspaper office for hours on end trying to figure out what Garth Miller was doing outside the Council boardroom *and* the State Trooper's office until I went mad. They didn't need the Chinese water torture with me. An unanswered question was going to work. Why hadn't I just asked him?

I know why.

He would have said something like: "I needed to get some information, why do you ask?" or "Because I wanted to, why are you here?"

None of those would have been the real answer, and I would have been left to have to give up the truth. I can't lie. I've tried. My face gets full of "lie alarms"; my eyes give me away. All of my body language works against me even as the words are coming out of my mouth.

"SHE'S LYING!" it screams.

I didn't want anyone to know I was working on finding out about the van for two reasons: the first is because so far, it was just curiosity, and that looked nosey, a very unflattering characteristic. The second reason was because if it turned out to be nothing, my boss would be mad I had used all of these resources for nothing.

I'd better just get to work and produce my stories or I

was going to be an unemployed non-liar and I can't think of a single job where that is a benefit. My editor Steve Hatcher looked in on me before lunch. He knows I have a strong work ethic and I will work through every meal if he's not careful. He pays me too little and gets too much out of me to let me die of starvation. There are only two reporters on staff, and the other guy only does sports. Gladys only does what she wants to, so that just leaves me for everything else.

"Do you need some lunch, or is your burnt toast still with you?" he grinned.

"How'd you know it was me?" I asked innocently.

"C'mon, just to show you there are no hard feelings, I'll spring for lunch."

"Also, you don't pay me enough to eat out."

"Righto, but you stay with me anyway, which just goes to show you don't think I should."

"Wait a minute, I..."

Steve grabbed me by the arm and my purse off my desk and hauled me out to his car. In this case, lunch out was the better part of valor.

In our little town you can eat at a "locals" restaurant, fast food or a cute little deli struggling to survive in a place that doesn't know what the word "deli" actually means. There's an ice cream counter at the local drug store, but they don't do lunch. Steve likes to eat at the "locals" restaurant because he likes to see and be seen. He is also not averse to listening in on conversations for the latest juicy comments. Journalism is a lot like gossip.

Whereas, I rely on my sources, who are in the know and

trust me, Steve prefers to skewer his sources with unreliable gossip. Even if he is wrong about what he heard, when he challenges his sources, his victims spill their guts trying to convince him of something else. Both our methods work, but obviously, Steve would have been a better match for Garth Miller this morning than I would have.

Yes, it was still bothering me. Okay, so I am a little on the obsessive side. When I start doodling Garth's name on things, then I'll know I need help.

"The Inn" was no more that, than the man in the moon. The name draws images of a quaint little roadside restaurant where the waitresses are sweet, motherly figures, maybe with a hint of a German accent, who tell you, you must eat your vegetables.

I don't even know why the people in this little town called this local restaurant "The Inn." There must have been some ancient tradition to it. There was no set of cottages attached to the restaurant. There wasn't even an old motel like the ones from the 50's where you parked your car outside your room and ate all your meals here.

The food was greasy and tasteless. They claimed home cooking, but if your mama had cooked like that, you would have run away. Why do we do things like this to ourselves? Well, of course …it was popular.

Remember the embarrassment you feel when you look back at your old high school annual? You can't believe you wore your hair like that, or actually had those clothes in your closet; worse, you put them on and wore them outdoors. What were you thinking? Oh right, …it was popular. I'm sure at the end of their lives, all the patrons of "The Inn" will say, "How could I have eaten at a place like that? Oh yeah, it was popular."

If you are a newly-inducted member of society in this town, you definitely would have been impressed with the clientele. Over here were the judges. There were the DA and the Assistant DA. The sheriff and his loyal deputies were over that way, his disloyal ones, back there.

The city police chief, Rufus Putnam, was sitting with - Oh No- yes, it was, the mayor, Garth Miller. Now this was too scary. Even if The Inn was the only place in town to eat, why was Garth eating at *this* particular time? Maybe I was just being paranoid. I tried not to look his way. Too late, he saw me and said something to the chief who looked deliberately at me and grinned. Ooh bad feeling, bad feeling.

I almost said to Steve, "Can I go walk on hot coals or something?"

Steve was too busy glad-handing the politicians and local celebrities, oh wait, the politicians *are* the local celebrities. He didn't notice my discomfort at all. Why hadn't I just stayed at the office with my burnt toast? Steve slid into a two-seater booth. Thank Goodness. I don't think I could have stood trying to make polite conversation with anyone around us. The tables were in close proximity to each other making it almost impossible not to overhear everything being said, or to converse with others even if only to say, "Sorry, I didn't mean to put my elbow in your salad."

Gussie, the waitress, handed us a couple of menus, smacked her gum in our faces and said, "Hurry up, this is the lunch crowd you know."

Perfect. Bad food *and* lousy service. Things just couldn't get any better.

And before you ask, "Gussie" is her real name. No kidding, her mama named her that. Just sat up after Gussie was born and said, "Now we'll have to get all gussied up for the Baptism." It stuck.

They thought she said, "Now we have to get Gussie up to the Baptist home." Before you taunt Gussie about how she got her name, you should know there is an "Ivy Cliff" in the neighborhood. That is her name. And there is a "Tiny" 'cause she was.

My own name might be the source of a comment or two, maybe even a snicker, but since no one, and I mean no one, is named Mildred anymore, and the people of this town thought it sounded too snooty anyhow, they took to my childhood nickname of "Mibbie." I can't claim royal connections like Princess Margaret Rose not being able to say Elizabeth and calling her later-to-be-queen sister "Lilibet, " but the principle was the same. My sister couldn't say my name, so I became Mibbie.

"Remind me to leave a big tip," Steve joked.

"That depends on if we live through this meal," I said.

"Ha! That was good, Mibbie. You're getting a sense of humor."

We scanned the menu and decided to risk our lives on a chicken sandwich. Steve reminded me the local chicken plant was being sued for the illegal use of steroids, and that, combined with The Inn's proclivity for making really bad food meant they would never be able to prosecute which one of them killed us. I coughed, and not from the food.

"Well, that's good enough for me," I said good-naturedly. "After all, we all have to die sometime."

"Funny, Mibs, you are full of them today."

I didn't really think I was being that funny, but Steve is my boss and you have to give them a little bit of encouragement along the way. About that time, Gussie slammed down two glasses of liquid. I'll bet it was supposed to be water, but it looked more like the stuff I'd seen in the storm drain outside the office yesterday.

Steve picked his up, "Cheers," he said and drank some until he grimaced. "Good old city water. You just can't beat it, no sir."

"Careful," I said, "You're starting to cut into my schtick."

"Ha!" Steve blasted out. "I swear Mib, you are going to have me in stitches."

It was a good thing Steve had me laughing because I didn't see when Garth made his way over to our booth with Chief Putnam in tow. If I had, my face would have betrayed me.

"SHE'S SCARED, SHE'S SCARED," it would have shrieked.

"So Steve, what's the top story this week?" Garth said smoothly. I lurched.

"Mayor poisoned at local restaurant," Steve grinned back.

"And Mibbie, what is your line these days?" Garth said

to me, his eyes drilling into mine like a super-powered nail gun. I liked it better when he knew I had something on him and gave me a wide berth.

"Oh, I have her working the customer service angle," Steve shot back. He laughed, but he was alone. He didn't notice, apparently, because he went on to say, "We've got Gussie up for a humanitarian award."

Garth was too busy trying to intimidate me to listen. The question was, why? What had I done to make him so edgy and downright hostile, not to mention the stalking thing, since just yesterday?

"Garth, when did you become interested in women? You haven't taken your eyes off my Mibbie since you walked up here. I know she's cute, but come on." Steve said without any tension in his voice. How does he do that?

The remark caught Garth off guard. He realized he had stared too long and said too much. This time he was the uncomfortable one, and I was glad. And the best part was that Steve had also made him forget about trying to get at me. When he spoke, Garth shifted his focus to Steve.

"I saw her talking to the sheriff yesterday after the council meeting. She was at the State Trooper's office this morning. Just wondered what that was all about," he said, trying to recover his composure by once again putting me on the spot.

I didn't say a word. I didn't have to, because Steve was enjoying himself.

"Well, I sent Mib over there to see if she could get them to start patrolling the streets of the city. Seems like our own police force is so overworked they can't get it all done. Just trying to lend a little helping hand to the city. What do you think, chief, need a little help?"

The police chief colored. He wasn't as competent as Garth in controlling the situation or his temper. His rage built from his collar up.

"Why you….," he started to say, but Garth put his hand on the chief's chest.

"Well now Steve, are you saying our city police don't do a good job?" Garth said, trying to lead Steve into a verbal trap. Steve wasn't biting.

"You don't want my opinion unless it's in my op-ed column. Just helping you out with your case of over-curiosity. Say Garth, when did Mibbie's activities interest you so much? Got a crush on her, do ya? Tell you what. Ring me when I get back to my office. I'll check her calendar without her knowing and you can show up wherever she is. How does that sound?" Steve crossed his arms and leaned back like he was fishing at his favorite hole and he knew he had just landed a granddaddy bass.

Garth was impressive. He didn't sputter. He didn't rage. He just smiled that icy cold smile of his and said, "You do that Steve." He quickly slithered away with the police chief behind him.

"Alright, give over. What was that all about?" Steve asked when Garth was gone. He leaned in with his elbows on the table.

"Can we talk about this later?" I pleaded. It was going to take all of my self-control to keep from shaking the water out of my glass with my unsteady hands when I downed the pond scum in my Sahara-like throat.

It didn't take the unappealing nature of the food when it arrived to ruin my appetite. Garth Miller had done that. Steve was worried.

"You've got to eat something. Your hands are trembling, and I know it can't all come from that run-in with Garth. Your blood sugar is low." At my forlorn look at him, he went on, "Oh, c'mon Mibs, don't let him bother you like that. Let Gussie bring you something else if this won't work." He gestured to the plate of food in front of me and grimaced.

He was right. I knew I needed to eat. I broke off a piece of the sandwich and put it in my mouth. It tasted like dust. I mean, it really tasted like dust, and it wasn't just because my mouth was dry from the surge of adrenaline now receding in my veins. The thought of how awful the food was here and that we were actually paying for it, made me give Steve a rueful smile. That was all he needed to resume his jocular performance.

Back at the office our stomachs were full, but suffering. Steve went to the kitchen for some Pepto-Bismol, then plopped himself down in my interview chair.

"Okay, now," he said perfunctorily and there was no way to avoid what he meant.

"Now this is scaring me Steve," I said. "All this is, is me checking on a car parked on the interstate. Billy and the troopers are helping me track it down. That's it. Why do you think Garth is so upset about that?"

"Is it his car?"

"No, in fact, it was stolen in Atlanta."

"There's something else. Are you telling me everything? I know how you love to protect that sheriff of yours."

"He's your sheriff too, Steve," I reminded him.

"Let's keep this straight. You are the one with loyalties. The only loyalty I have is to this newspaper. That includes you. If I have to take you down for a good story, I'll do it. So if you and your sheriff are cooking outside the kitchen you better give it to me now."

While I could have kissed him at lunch, I could have slapped him just then.

"There's nothing else that I know of. That doesn't mean something won't show up, but I'll let you know if it does. Thanks for the guard dog routine at lunch, but you're off base if you think the sheriff and I would work on something and I wouldn't tell you. You know how honest I am."

Steve must have felt the need to apologize. "Sorry Mib. You know I trust you. It's just that I don't trust anybody else. You have to be the one to get it. Look, let's just leave it at this. Dig around if you want, but if it becomes something. Let me know. Don't get me into a corner. I'm not trying to be mean or anything, but if you hang me out to dry, you'll pay."

Steve patted me on the arm and got up and left. It didn't sit well with me. I don't like being threatened, even if I am wrong. But I wasn't wrong here. I kept trying to tell myself that Steve's reaction was only because of Garth's. What was that all about?

I hammered out two more stories and looked at the clock. It was time to go see my daughter conduct her swim lessons. Another cough reminded me of my mortality.

The local college had an indoor pool and that meant swim lessons could be given at any time of year. It was a good supplement to a high schooler's income and good training for Elizabeth's future teaching career.

Although I had my doubts about whether I wanted my child to suffer the slings and arrows of outrageous education policies, one thing was certain, it was in her blood, so she was trying teaching out. Besides, journalism wasn't much of a step up at this point, or at least I didn't think so today.

I was picking Elizabeth up from her job there.

I slid onto one of the benches beside the pool deck of the college's indoor pool. I was surrounded by perfectly coiffed, manicured, fashion-plated moms. In our small town, there are all kinds of people, and these women formed what could be called the social mom network, or, the nest of vipers that every woman hates or fears. Like the patrons of The Inn who took their lives in their hands to eat there, just so they could rub shoulders with the local celebrities, these women loved to play at being snobs.

I'm not sure what they are so proud of. It's just a small town. But isn't that how small town big shots are? "I'm so important, because of my name, my family status, how big my house is ...".

I'm not a slob, but you could tell by the way their eyes raked over me I was considered something less acceptable than a stopped-up commode before a big dinner party.

One of them always tries it. Her conscience will bother her because she sees the disdain the rest of the moms treat me with, so Miss Do-Gooder will say, "And which one is your child?" thinking I will point to a tattered rag-a-muffin with crooked teeth and stringy hair. She will feel great pity for me and smile consolingly for the sorrow of being the mother of the ugliest child in the swim class.

Then she can look at her friends and smile patronizingly that at least she took an interest in the poor little mite. I love this.

I sit up straight, face her with a piercing gaze and say, "She's the teacher."

The blood drains out of her face. She realizes that my child, my flesh and blood has power over hers. I am, in fact, not the mother of the ugly duckling, but of the swan, and the chief swan, at that. My child is great. As if on cue, she halts the class and waves to me. I am the acknowledged maven of the swim lesson entourage. I try not to be smug. That's wrong.

Chapter 7

After swimming lessons, I kissed my child and told her I was ready to go home. I forgot for a moment that she is a teenager.

"Mom, you know I told you we were going to have a cook-out for Brian's birthday," she said. "We're going to meet at Sarah's house."

"Oh yeah," I said. "I forgot."

Now I made an "A" in Guilt 101 under my mama's brilliant tutelage, so I could have guilted her into letting me come along, or not staying out late and coming home to spend some time with me, but I am a nice person. I let it go.

"How late then?"

"Not bad, say 10:00?"

I have really good kids. They go where they say they are going; they do what they say they are going to do. I don't have to wait at the door with a breathalyzer and a cup to do drug and alcohol tests. The real reason I hesitate is that I am coming to the point of the empty nest. Even though there is no empirical evidence to support the idea that there really is such a syndrome, I'm not sure what it will mean to no longer have my children in my life, but living their own. This one is a high school senior.

I have Emily coming up as a junior and my son will soon graduate from college. In two years, there won't be any more

Friday night football games, weeknight volleyball, basketball, soccer or softball games. No hustle and bustle of youth, just boring, old me. The kids have worried about this more than I have. They are always trying to "hook me up," the new teen phrase for dating. I suspect, though, that the word "hook" has less than moral connotations.

I tried not to sigh when I told her to go on and I'd see her later. It isn't that I need company with five chickens, four cats, three dogs and a duck. I headed home for an old movie and fondue. Good old comfort food, though I doubt most people mean something as pretentious as French cuisine when they say that.

****

When I got my first answering machine, I thought it was like a gift. I would run to it to see who had called while I was gone. I'm still a kid at heart about hearing messages, and I am probably the last surviving person in the world to have an answering machine. That's because where I live, cell service is non-existent, and I am probably the least surviving person to have a landline, hence the need for an answering machine.

I'm glad I was born in this era with dishwashers, cell phones, and all kinds of gadgets that make life more interesting or more horrifying if you are their slave. Technology can ensnare you and steal your self-reliance. My problem is that it moves faster than I do. I stopped trying to keep up, and I'm resting on the side of the metaphorical road, until I find I need any of the new stuff. So far, I don't. One of the delightful things about growing older is finding out how very little you need.

Today the "F" was flashing on the answering machine, meaning "full". Also meaning I had once again forgotten to delete some messages. I picked up a pen so I could write down what I was sure I wouldn't remember:

"Hey Mibbie, I've got the owner of that van's name. Call me back and I'll give it to you"

Billy.

"Ms. Wright, this is Missy from Dr. Bergman's office, could you call us at your earliest convenience. The number here is 555-6137."

Uh-Oh, doctor's office. Forgot about that visit.

"Ms. Wright, this is Gayle at Sheriff Bartlett's office. He asked me to call you and let you know that he and Mr. Treadwell will be meeting at 8:00 A.M. tomorrow morning at Mr. Treadwell's office. Can you be there? If so, they said there is no need to call, just be there. If not, please call them and let them know."

"Hey mom, just checking in. Why are you never home? I know you're not out on a date. Oh sorry, you could be out on a date, but usually you're not. What I mean is…Okay, I know what you're thinking, 'I taught my son better than that.' No insult meant. Call me when you get home."

Ah, the man in my life, my son.

"Mom, I'm studying with Casey. Be home at 9:00."

Other girl child, Emily.

"Ms. Wright, your book is in. Could you come by during library hours tomorrow and pick it up?"

Faithful librarian.

Hang up.

Hang up.

Hang up.

Maybe those were sales calls. Or maybe it was someone trying to see if I was home. Garth?

The only one that bothered me was the one from Dr. Bergman's office. Since I had been nagged by my children to go and see about this bothersome cough, though actually, I think it was more bothersome to them than to me, I hadn't given much thought to the idea I might really be sick.

Dr. Bergman wanted to look a little deeper than just listening to my chest. He'd heard some rattling and had ordered an x-ray. His office's phone call meant he was requiring me to come back whether I wanted to or not. I'm of the "If it isn't broken don't fix it" school of health. I just don't want to know. But the die was cast and I was going to have to see what was causing this cough.

I went outside with the good intention of taking a walk to offset my guilt for eating fondue for dinner. The crisp clean air of April is conducive to healthy thoughts and actions. My home is located in a remote area with lots of woods, paths made by my own dogs and the wildlife that bountifully surrounds us.

My road used to be dirt until the County Commissioners figured out that I had a little power through the publicity I garnered as a local informant. Just before the elections year before last, they had the paving boys come out and give the road the once-over. Since elections are held every four years, I wasn't sure when the next paving would take place. I mean, thank you for the start on the paving, but if you never finish it, what is the point?

They stagger the offices that are up for re-election so that the entire group of elected officials is not changing offices at one time. I think this is wise. You can't have *everyone* be new to the job. But if you are looking for political favors, you better hope it is your guy's turn to be elected.

I wouldn't have minded the road staying rustic out here except that it invited unsavory characters and their even more unsavory behavior: young people looking for a place to drink without the prying parental eyes; young lovers looking for a place to experiment with their newly-discovered anatomical differences; reprobates like Bruce Tyner; hunters who were sure the fabled white stag existed in my lowly woods and therefore, shot randomly at anything that moved, including me; and the four-legged or wheeled adventurers (horseback riders and four-wheel riders) looking for wide stretches of countryside to ride for hours and hours.

Since I'd heard four wheelers buzzing up and down the power line last night, I decided to point myself in that direction. I could accomplish two things at once, find the errant travelers and shoo them off the premises while giving myself some much-needed exercise.

The whole world beyond my front porch was a young, translucent green. Wild flowers competed for the stage, each taking her time to flower and gracefully wave at her audience as she pirouetted with the wind. I revel in my peaceful existence here and seek to protect it. That is what made me so determined today to seek out the offending clamor causers and put a stop to them.

I got precisely fifty feet before beginning to wheeze and cough. Nope, no walk tonight. My lungs simply would not permit it. The four-wheelers had another day of reprieve from my behavior modification efforts.

Good thing the library had called. A good book is a wonderful distraction for whatever keeps your mind upset. Parked cars and trespassers would be put to rest when I settled down to the book I'd be getting from the library tomorrow, but a good movie would do for now. Tonight's special was *It Happened One Night* with Claudette Colbert and Clark Gable.

Bright and early the next day, I popped out of bed. Actually I was very weary, but I told myself I popped, just to use mind over matter. The brain is a marvelous thing for convincing us of things otherwise untrue. I was anxious to meet Billy and Marvin and see what they had for me. The great thing about being a reporter is that you can slide on a pair of khakis, a white collared shirt and a blazer and you look downright professional. I grabbed my camera bag and my favorite pen.

If you are a writer, one of the most important things you have is the "just right" pen. For me it is a Uni-ball Vision Fine Line. I love the juxtaposition of the very black, solid ink on a very white, lined background. Armed with my recording devices, I coasted into the State Trooper's office parking lot at 7:55. I never like to be early somewhere. It is a waste. Instead, I like being just on time.

The doors to the public were not open, but I knew the night code. It wasn't like it wasn't public knowledge, so don't think I had special privileges. Besides, what burglar was going to break into a law enforcement office that was manned 24 hours a day? Okay dumb question; they do have a show called *Stupidest Criminals* don't they?

Billy got up when I walked in like the gentleman he is. "Hey kid," he said in greeting. Marvin smiled that devastatingly brilliant smile of his. Am I a lucky girl or what?

"The owner of that van is Marvella Sanchez," Marvin said. "She reported it stolen last Thursday. Says she thinks she knows who took it but doesn't want to press charges. We know a guy over there and he said that Marvella is clear for her green card, but that she is in a bad spot and he thinks somebody without the proper credentials took it. She doesn't want to pursue it because there will be retribution. She is a single mom with kids, just trying to make it. The police figured out what was going on by talking to her. They have their suspicions, too, about who took it.

"They followed up. The guy they think took it is Delago Fuentez. Had a green card, but it looked wrong and no real ID. He hasn't been around for a while. We have his records for some criminal activity. Thing is, they couldn't make the case, so they had to let him go. And his green card seems to be fake, so they think someone is working the system for him.

"We got the report back from forensics. Marvella was happy to cooperate for that part of the investigation since it would not involve anyone else, so we got her and her kid's fingerprints eliminated from the mix. That left us with Fuentez. There's a match. We also were able to make him on the Hardee's food contents.

"So we know who stole it, we know where he took it. The question is, where is he, and why did he come here? Did he mean to stop here, or was this just a stopping-off point for Marvella's van? I know you're going to ask, so through Victim's Services we got her another van to use until we are finished with hers."

He knows me well.

"No blood, no ballistics, nothing else to indicate foul play of any kind."

"So where do you go from here?"

"Well, that's just it, until a development comes up, there isn't anywhere to go. As it is, we just wait."

I told them about lunch yesterday and what Steve had said about us having a story and not letting him know. Marvin smiled about Garth's reaction. Billy didn't.

"He's just messing with you Mibbie," Marvin soothed.

"Uh-Uh," Billy said. "He usually just ignores her. Have you got anything going on with him, Marvin?"

"No," said Marvin. "Even if I did, it wouldn't be political. You know he wants that Senate seat to be vacated in November right? Maybe he thinks he can ride on Mibbie's news stories like he thinks you did. If she gives him any press time, it will look good for him. He knows she wouldn't do it unless it was legit, so maybe he wants to intimidate her into making him look good for the public."

What Marvin said made sense. Still, that woman's intuition thing kept nagging at me that there was more to his following me around than just some free press, and Billy frowned. I knew he was thinking that, too.

"Maybe," was all he said.

I had a coughing fit, and both men looked concerned.

"Better get that checked out, Mib" said Billy.

"On it," I managed to croak, in between hacking.

I left and walked over to the office. That is another great thing about where I work. It is centrally located right next to the courthouse, city hall, police station, sheriff's department and trooper's office, so I could leave my car in one spot and still get where I needed to go. I had a beauty pageant to cover and a visiting author coming to the local library. While I was there I could pick up my book.

Out of the corner of my eye, I saw Garth Miller's very distinguishable BMW coasting to a park in the city hall parking lot. He is the only person I know who can afford to drive one, or who would drive one in a small town like Morton. He got out and stood looking at me for a long time. The courthouse would open at 9:00, but why was Garth there so early? He usually kept banker's hours, if he came to City Hall at all.

Steve was in his office on the phone with someone when I arrived. By the sound of it, it was not a pleasant conversation for either of them. Better get out the Pepto with a big spoon. I tiptoed to my computer to start cropping pictures to go with my stories.

I could tell when Steve got off the phone. First, there

was the slam of the phone onto the cradle. I'd bet we were going to be ordering a new one. Then there was the slam of his chair against the wall when he got up. Call the drywallers. Then there was the slam of his leg against the front office counter. Oops, expletives too numerous to count. Call the EMT's. Good thing I had put out the Pepto, or we might have been replacing the refrigerator door. I knew better than to say anything. Just keep quiet and keep working.

Steve came in. He stood there with his eyes on fire, his chest heaving. I thought I might be the one who was going to get slammed next, and I could feel my heart starting to thud. Different escape routes rose up in my mind. The easiest escape was the door, but I had just settled on the window escape route next to my chair for my Houdini disappearing trick when Steve decided to speak.

"That was Senator Hughes," he said, trying to keep his voice in a measured tone.

Whew, it wasn't about me after all. The good senator was a consummate politician. He was sticky and slimy like a slug you step on in your bare feet. You think you'll never get the nasty stuff off you. I always had to take a shower after I talked to him. I knew better than to ask what he had said because that was going to unleash a dam, and I hadn't brought my swimsuit. After a long silence, Steve tried to speak. It came out like gears grinding. He left the room. I heard him get a drink of water. He came back.

"He wants us to do a story about Garth. He didn't say why, but I know it is for this upcoming Senate race in November. I told him I'd be happy to do a story on him when

Garth did something noteworthy. Hughes says Garth is noteworthy; he doesn't have to *do* anything, all that nonsense about Garth being a young progressive. Like Garth didn't milk that for everything when he came into office. Like the people of this county read things like *Newsweek* if they did do a story on him. It's old news and you know how I hate that. I'm not going to rehash it." Steve was clenching his teeth.

Uh-oh, I knew what was coming next. Don't do it Steve, don't do it.

"So I told him you would see what you could find out."

Oh Steve, you did it. Can I fall to the floor dead now? Should I tell him about my impending visit to the doctor to solicit some sympathy? Where was the Hari Kari knife when you needed it? Nope, nothing to save me.

"Can I just do an update on what his original campaign was?" I ventured.

Steve looked at me like I was next on his "To Murder" list.

"I said, we don't rehash the news. Didn't you hear me Mibbie?" Steve growled.

"Oh yeah, I forgot, sorry," The "this paper is my mistress" thing. You give the wife a sensible wool coat, but the mistress gets the new fur. Well, this was going to be interesting, or difficult, or both. At least Marvin's assessment of Garth's interest in me was confirmed and I could put the issue out of my mind.

Don't you hate it when you have to do distasteful things? Speaking of that, the next thing I was going to do was go see the doctor. Might as well do all the bad stuff at once.

Chapter 8

I did as much as I could that morning because I was not going to be coming back to the office for a while. It was only Wednesday, but I had pneumonia. It doesn't sound nearly as pathetic as something life threatening, but it didn't matter. Nothing was going to get me out of having to do a story on Garth, short of death, that is. And although I keep telling my children that I am worth more to them dead than alive, they insist I hang around for a while longer.

Fortunately, I had gotten my new book from the library, something for me to do while I was recuperating. Steve insisted I could write my stories at home, and email them in. Didn't the fact that the doctor had said, "Rest" mean anything to this workaholic?

I had just pulled off my interstate exit, breathing in what little lovely, new spring air I could fit into my clogged lungs when the most revolting smell you can imagine grabbed my nose and wrenched it into knots. I started to wind the window up, but when I pushed the button, I heard a grinding noise instead.

"Oh no," my famous last words for most of my life.

Yep, the window of my car was broken. My brain said, "Drive away quickly." My woman's intuition said, "What is that awful smell?" and "You'd better find out." Okay, I was sick. Could I use that for the reason behind what I did next?

No, I am just like a cat, overly curious, and one day it is going to kill me. I pulled over.

Following the smell was not hard. It got worse as I moved from the exit ramp toward the entrance ramp on the other side of the interstate. I decided to get back in my car and drive. I was too tired to chase anything on foot if I didn't have to. On the opposite side where the entrance ramp was, I pulled over to the side of the road. This was where the Aerostar van had been parked. It was gone now, since Marvin's guys had towed it in for investigation, but oil spots and tire tread marks indicated where it had been. I got out of the car and took my jacket off, putting it up to my nose. Better to get chilled than to subject myself to this smell.

Off the road the trees grew thick, but that had also kept the underbrush from growing up, so traveling towards the awful smell wasn't so bad. Deeper into the thicket, however, the ground began to rise and I knew I was at the base of the mountain. Good thing it was still daylight or the hiking could have been treacherous with rocks and crevices all around. The heavy tree cover made it almost dark.

Looking back, I'm not sure if I realized it was Delago Fuentez when I saw him. He'd been there a while, and his body was bloated. He had also been ravaged by the wild animals in the area. I can tell you it was a sight that made me feel like I had visited Hell. Of course it made me sick. Thank God Gayle answered the phone when I called Billy. I think I would have fainted trying to convince Bruce Tyner of the proper grammar to put me through.

Chapter 9

A doctor once laughed at me for asking him not to give me antibiotics.

"They make me sleepy," I said.

His condescending laughter was exceeded only by his sardonic reply: "Antibiotics have many side-effects, but making you sleepy is not one of them."

I heard his laughter as I struggled awake from the antibiotics I was taking for the horrible, stuffy thing now residing in my chest. I'd been asleep for three days. I knew, rather than saw, that someone was standing at the end of my bed. My son had come home from college to check on me. He has never been given to much sympathy for the sick bed.

Once, when I was in bed with a temperature of 104, he threw me a bottle of aspirin and told me, "Okay, take two of these and come on outside."

Today, maybe he'd be at least a little more sympathetic. "What's this about you finding dead bodies instead of getting home in time to make dinner," I heard his familiar voice say. Nope. Clearly, we were going to have to work on that part of his character.

My son.

God love him, and especially the woman he marries. Southern women say "God love him" whenever they are trying to show extraordinary patience toward someone. If they say, "Bless his heart" you know they have just skewered someone on the gossip grill.

"I didn't mean to be finding dead bodies. It just turned up. Has Billy called?"

"Yes, and he had the same question. Am I supposed to tell your boss you are too sick to type your stories, but not too sick to play detective?"

"I'm not playing detective."

"Is that what I'm supposed to say, or do you really believe that?"

"Can I help it nobody but me has a sense of smell? You can't think I really wanted to see that, can you?"

"C'mon Mom, save it for the interrogation you are going to have to go through. I know what you are like. I told you all those *Mystery's* on PBS were going to catch up to you."

Gee, I was hoping he wasn't right. Could I really get into trouble for what I had done? Maybe coming out of an antibiotic induced coma wasn't such a good idea after all. I took a ragged breath and turned over to let my son know I wasn't going to be waking up any time soon. Two more days should do it.

Whether we like it or not, the world keeps turning. Let some tragedy strike your life and just as surely some telephone solicitor is going to call you and act like nothing has happened. Or get yourself into an accident with your neck wrenched and blood everywhere and the emergency room nurse insists on having you fill out paperwork for three hours to determine if you have insurance.

So it came as no surprise when all three of my children were standing at the foot of my bed wanting, respectively: dinner; to know if I was going to talk to Steve; and to find out if it was okay to have the soccer team over to spend the night on Friday.

I figured I'd better talk to Steve or he'd be over at my house himself. I told them to fend for themselves for dinner and they could entertain the soccer team next Friday night, and to tell Steve he could talk to me on Wednesday morning. Steve insisted on talking to me now.

"You don't sound that sick. Are you sure you can't come in?"

"Steve, do you want to put an ad in your newspaper for another reporter?"

"No."

"Well then, you can't kill the one you have. If you really don't believe me I'll have them fax over a copy of the x-rays. I really am sick. I promise. However, if you don't stop making me try to prove it, I will die and you will be stuck doing the story on Garth, yourself."

Silence.

I think I made my point.

"Okay Mibs. Did you take any pictures of Fuentez? How about typing up what you know. We have an exclusive on this; did I tell you? Billy has agreed to release the facts to us first since you discovered the body." Ah, the prattling of a happy and contented boss. Maybe I wasn't going to be in trouble after all.

Nope, too soon for that good thought. The next phone

call was from the DA's office wanting to know when I could come in for a statement. Did I have an attorney, no, better get one. This was murder and I needed to be ruled out as a suspect.

Wait a minute, what happened to doing the right thing as a good citizen? Sorry, these are the rules. Was I feeling well enough for next Thursday's Coroner's hearing? No, I started to say, but I realized I had slept through the weekend and would still have another three days to recuperate. As tired as I was, I should be able to swing it, then come home for a rest.

Of course, as soon as Steve heard I was up, he'd be after me to come into the office. Bull terriers have nothing on my boss. Why did I put up with such abuse?

Time for another nap.

Billy's phone call an hour later was a welcome one. He was the first person I had talked to who actually wanted to know how I was, first. Business second.

"Good thing you got to him when you did Mib. We might never have found him. We know he was murdered, but we're still trying to figure out by who and why. We're waiting until you're on your feet so you can give us some specific information, but we have a lot more because of you." What a nice guy.

"The DA's office called. They act like I am the one who did something wrong."

"Don't worry about it. They treat everyone that way. If you didn't do it, it ensures you'll be cooperative. If you did, they've done their job to get you. Try to get some rest so you can think clearly. Any information you can give them, or us, is going to help solve this case."

I felt another nap coming on.

You can always tell when something in my life is improving, because that is when everything else thinks it has the right to go wrong. In this case, it was my health that was improving.

"Mom, the dishwasher won't turn on when I push the button."

"Mom, why won't the oven come on? The top part of the stove is working."

Yep, life was getting back to normal.

Chapter 10

I typed up the story on what I had seen and met with Billy on Wednesday. We knew Fuentez had stolen the green van two weeks ago and the coroner had determined that the cause of death was a gunshot wound at point blank range. Forensics said the murder had taken place Tuesday night a week ago. A week in the woods was all it took to get him into the state I'd found him in.

It was the reverse of fall's Indian Summer when the weather was cool at night and hot all day. April had given us a couple of warm spring days to herald summer while still holding us tightly in her cold grasp. The daytime heat had helped speed along the decomposing process, but not in enough time that Delago's body had been detected when they picked up the van.

Nobody had figured out yet what Fuentez was doing in this part of the world and why he chose to fatefully park the stolen van where he would lose his life. Billy and his team of investigators were scouring the vehicle for any DNA evidence to see if they could pick up anything else that the first search hadn't revealed in light of finding the body.

Like the wheels of justice, the collection process of the tiny little details of a case takes a long time. Most young people get into the criminal justice aspect of the law for the excitement. They get out of it because they discover quickly enough that putting all that data together is not only time-consuming and tedious, it is also not glamorous.

I think television and movies have put to rest most of the daily living in this world. Youth today think doctors really do have more time for love affairs than they do for practicing medicine. They think lawyers spend more time on theatrics than they do on research. They think all it takes is a pretty face, an average voice, and a modicum of talent on the high school football field to launch them into a high-paying career. Poor kids. The illusion is short-lived.

Even my time as a journalist has taken its toll. Yes, it is fun to go places and be recognized, but it is also not much fun to be the target of hate mail from people you don't even know who are too cowardly to tell you what they think to your face. As far as writing a story, I know to be very careful of my facts. The old adage that: "Figures don't lie, but liars sure can figure," is true for information, too. Even a well-meaning journalist can ruin someone's life if they don't get the facts straight. I'm not so worried about what Steve thinks as I am about the responsibility of getting it right.

I felt that way when I was a teacher. It made me angry when teachers got tired of teaching, but the retirement was too good to pass up. They stayed on in that classroom, wasting those kid's time just so they could fatten up their retirement check. The minds of those kids were stagnant. Their time was spent and you never get that back. I think it's criminal.

The next day was my appointment at the DA's office for my statement. Fortunately for me, when Judge Bill Tarleton heard I was in the midst of a criminal investigation and needed legal counsel, he sent over one of his lawyers from his old firm. He is good to me this way. When he found out I didn't have a will and knew I wouldn't spend money on that when I had tuition due, he wrote one up for me.

"It's just good lawyerin, Mibbie," he had said when he dropped it off, as if his gift to me was part of his job and I had actually paid him for it. Good men are hard to find, but they are out there. My new buddy was just out of law school, but I knew Judge Tarleton had thought long and hard before he hired him. After all, this was his daddy's firm and Judge Tarleton wasn't going to let some whippersnapper, fly-by-the-seat-of-his-pants- youngster, come in and desecrate it. I felt well represented.

I gave my statement in the presence of my lawyer who nodded and scratched notes on a legal pad. Don't you just love legal pads? There is so much room to write. It took me the longest time to figure out that they call them "legal" for a reason. I use them prodigiously.

The DA ascertained I was, in fact, not a criminal, and therefore could go about my business. They were not forthcoming with any other information and the reporter in me stung. I wanted to ask some questions, but I wasn't there in an official capacity. I would have to make a return trip.

Steve was so excited to have me back, he let me go home afterwards for a nap. The story Billy and Marvin had helped me pull together and the fact that we had an exclusive made Steve less perverse in his demands on my time. Except for the fact that I still had to do the Garth Miller story, I was in pretty good shape.

Chapter 11

It must be the writer in me that loves to make up stories. I can't help it. Watching people makes me wonder what their lives are like. Sometimes I catch myself staring at people trying to figure them out, which can be misconstrued as being rude. A couple of ugly gestures from my subjects cured me of that trait. I learned to watch people surreptitiously.

I also have an inordinately strong curiosity meter, so I like to observe what people are doing around me. This would be a very good thing if I were the next target of a mugger. I would detect he was taking an interest in me and would be able to deflect his attack. However, since I am not typically the target of a mugger, my curiosity meter usually serves to just entertain me.

I was sitting under a tree on the local college campus waiting for Elizabeth to finish teaching her swim lessons at the college pool, when I noticed a small silver coupe slowly glide, then park, near a wooded area. A boy got out and left a girl in the car. He was dark-headed, wiry; she was blonde, but from my view, I couldn't see much else. He disappeared down a makeshift road and was gone for a while. When Elizabeth showed up, she whistled for me.

"I don't respond to whistles anymore," I said. "I'm too old."

She just smiled.

"What are you doing? You got your pants all dirty sitting on the ground." Makes you wonder who the parent is in this relationship.

"What would make somebody go down that dirt road?" I asked.

She looked in the direction I pointed, and asked, "Guy?" I nodded.

"Well, the obvious then."

"Nope, gone too long. And if the other thing was necessary, don't you think he would have used the fast food restaurant's?"

"You're so nosey."

"Don't be mean. It doesn't look good on you. Really, what do you think is going on there?"

"Mom, if you think there is anything illicit going on you should call the police."

I should have, and I knew it, but I couldn't help myself. I already had a good story line going on in my head, and I couldn't let it go. People are generally logical, unless they are under the influence of drugs and alcohol. Either this guy was under the influence, or there was something more than met the eye. Elizabeth was right. I should have called the police. I had no right to find out what was going on …unless…

Elizabeth grabbed my arm. "Look Inspector Clouseau, you just march yourself over here to your car and stop this nonsense."

I hesitated. "Okay," I said. "I'll just wait here until he

comes out again."

"And do what, follow him? Are you aware that that is breaking the law?"

She was right. This whole Wild West maverick thing was going to get me in trouble. Why can't I learn to mind my own business, or at least ask for help? I needed help. What I also needed was to find out whose jurisdiction this area was. If it was the city's, there was no way I was going to call anybody. I would surely end up in jail then. I dialed Billy's office.

"Sheriff's Department" sang Gayle. Good, I stood a chance here.

"Gayle, it's Mibbie. Is Billy in?" She patched me through.

"Hey, Mib. What's up?" he asked when he came on the line.

"Billy, don't think I'm insane, but I need a guy checked out."

"Do you mean DMV?"

"No, ITW."

"What?"

"Sorry, 'In The Woods'. What I mean is, there is this guy, a kid really, down here by the woods next to the college and he is walking down this dirt road. Why?"

"Did you ask him?" I could hear the smile on his face.

"Okay stop. He has been gone longer than the 'call of nature' time frame. What is he doing down that road?"

"Whoa girl, are you getting carried away? You find one dead guy and now you are a detective."

69

"C'mon Billy, when have you ever known me to get carried away?" I heard an intake of breath. He was about to tell me. "Forget that. Just trust me, okay? Whose jurisdiction is this?"

"Well, ours if it's in the woods. On campus it's the campus police, then after that it becomes rural. That's ours. A little further back, close to the interstate and Marvin could help us."

"Is there anybody you could send over to check this out? The guy has been gone a while and I expected him back at any moment if there was legitimate reason for him to be down that road. I just know there is something to this." I could hear Billy using his mike.

"Okay, I'm sending Fred over. He likes you, so he shouldn't give you any trouble when this turns out to be a false alarm."

About ten minutes later a deputy car cruised up to the road and Fred Mabry got out. Fred was an old country boy who believed in doing the right thing. He was one of the only deputies who had stuck by Billy when things were bad. He had my utmost admiration and respect because he wasn't afraid to be on the side of right, even if it meant he stood alone.

The guy in the woods had still not emerged, and I could see the girl in the passenger side of the parked car jerk her head to attention when she caught sight of Fred. He spoke to her, and then headed down the road. She got out of the car as soon as he was out of sight. She looked around furtively, and began to run. I wasn't sure what to do. The justice side

70

of me wanted to chase her down to ask her questions.

The child on my side said, "Don't even think about it! I know exactly what you are going to do. If you chase her …and do I have to remind you, you are not a policeman…you will be breaking another law. Mom, will you stop trying to go to jail!"

By this time the girl was well onto campus and about to get lost in the crowd of students. Elizabeth read my mind. It helped that I was squirming in her grasp.

"Get your notebook. Make a list of details. You know your memory is going." I did not think this was a good time to be reminding me of the aging process and the toll it was taking on me. She was right, though. Nothing can replace good notes, as any self-respecting journalist will tell you. Suddenly, Elizabeth lurched. She pointed to the departing figure.

"You're in luck mom, that's Jessica. She's saying something to the girl, and she will be able to tell you if she knows her." Sure enough, Jessica Hanover, one of the girls from last year's senior class, turned and watched the girl tearing past her. This was good.

While we had been watching the retreating accomplice, Fred must have been dealing with something. He was still gone. Elizabeth knew I would want to go down the road to see what was going on, but instead she convinced me to see if I could find Jessica to find out more about the errant child who had involved herself in something obviously illegal.

I didn't blame her really. It was easy for young people to get caught up in things without realizing the consequences. Just watch an episode of *Cops* for a dose of that reality.

The reasonable side of me decided to go find Jessica and talk to her. The instinct side of me was desperate to find out what Fred had found out. Reason first, then instinct.

Nope, instinct won out; I headed towards the dirt road. Elizabeth caught up to me. We walked to the parked car sitting there, along with the cruiser. No sign of Fred or the guy. Elizabeth read my mind again. This motherhood tie was beginning to be a burden.

"You're not going down there. If Fred can't handle whatever he finds, you sure can't. Better call Billy," she said.

I did, and I could hear the grimness in his voice when he was unable to raise Fred on his walkie-talkie. He would be coming himself. I felt awful. I couldn't blame anybody but myself for getting one of Billy's best guys in a pickle. The worst thing was that I knew what he would say: "All in the line of duty, Mib." Didn't help. I still felt miserable.

Billy was there in less than five minutes. He had brought backup, and I was glad to see Bruce wasn't among them. As they started down the road, I took my place alongside Billy, my usual spot when I was accompanying him on police business as a journalist.

We have a great relationship that way. He has always been very open and public about how police business works and was the first law enforcement officer who actually brought me along on investigations. I saw some things I didn't want to see, which is natural when you are dealing with the lawless side of life.

I don't know when I will ever learn. I knew I would be sorry to see what was down that road. As humans we just can't seem to listen to our own good reasoning skills. There was Fred, lying prone, a pool of blood forming at his side.

Chapter 12

Billy wasn't smiling when he said, "When should I start worrying that there are so many bodies showing up near you?"

Under any other circumstance it might have been funny, but Fred was one of his best men and Billy didn't take his getting shot lightly. We were sitting in his office after dealing with the crush of business related to getting Fred to the hospital.

"Do you know, yet, who shot him?"

"We have some leads, but I really can't say anything." He was starting to sound like I was just another reporter who couldn't be trusted. I didn't like that. We have always had a level of trust between us that exceeded our business relationship. Could this incident have destroyed that?

"Do you mean you can't say anything because it is too tentative, or you can't say anything because I am a reporter and you don't want to be quoted?"

Billy visibly eased his shoulders down. I could tell he was releasing some anger.

"I know this is not your fault. I know that Fred was just doing what he should have done given these circumstances. It just looks bad that we were following a line from you, and he ends up hurt."

"Well, let's take a different tack on this. Instead of

saying you were following a line from me, which I have to admit, even liking myself as I do, sounds like a bad idea, why don't you just say that you were following up on some suspicious behavior, and, as it turns out, it was more than just suspicious. That kid was clearly up to something and one way or another you were going to find out about it because you're a good cop. It just happens that Fred got caught in the cross-fire."

I wasn't sure this would make Billy feel any better. I know I didn't.

****

I love to visit hospitals at night. There is something so peaceful about that big, lighted building standing stark against the dark night where ailing people are getting care from quietly shuffling nurses. The perky little gift shop is closed and the real business of the place is being attended to.

My visit tonight was not so much for Fred, but for his family whom I knew would be in the intensive care waiting room. Once, when my mother was dying, someone was kind enough to send a care basket full of goodies: gum, drinks, mouth lozenges, magazines and other comforting things. There is nothing lonelier than sitting outside intensive care waiting for the golden hour to visit your loved one. I hoped Fred's family wouldn't despise the sight of me and blame me for them being in that position, now.

Fred's wife Ruth looked the part of someone in a stressful situation. The lines around her eyes were strong and dark. Her mouth was a tight, grim line. Fred was an older father and his daughters were also there with their husbands.

75

Their kids must have been at home with the other grandparents.

Sometimes words are not a good idea. I walked over to one of the girls and handed her the basket. Her look told me she was angry. Maybe not at me, but there was no reason not to think so since I was pretty sure that the gossip around the department had made me responsible for their daddy's condition. I turned to Ruth who hugged me tightly. Was it forgiveness or relief? She knew I wanted to know how Fred was doing.

"You know my old buzzard," she said. "He's too tough for these stupid thugs to kill. He's gotta internal injury from the bullet passin' through the muscle tissue in his abdomen, but the punk didn't know how to shoot too good. That's in our favor. Not in his though, 'cause the minute Fred gets up outta that bed, he's comin' after him."

It all sounded so hopeful, and I searched her eyes for evidence that she wasn't just trying to be brave, that she really believed all that she was saying. She smiled for the first time. It was a weary smile that told me she had faced the truth. She probably wouldn't see Fred back on duty. He would take a desk job or retire. He had escaped death. It looked as though Fred and Ruth had forgiven me. In time, maybe their girls would, too. Visiting intensive care patients is for the family, so I said my goodbyes and left.

I vowed then and there to do something to find the guy who had done this. I was going to redeem myself with Billy by picking up the lead I had, and I was going to track down the criminal who had put Fred on the retirement track.

My next visit was to see Jessica Hanover to find out more about the blonde girl who had been in the car when Fred took his fateful walk. I would do that first thing in the morning.

Chapter 13

Jessica Hanover was one of those all-star kids. She had been a student-athlete all through high school and was a part of just about every club, was in the marching band when she wasn't playing a sport, and managed a 3.8 average. It was natural that she would be a pick for the local college.

They scout the resident high school routinely for the top kids, having an advantage over other colleges because they can court good students early. Their admissions officer is a frequent guest to the high school campus. Although they offer a great education, I sometimes think it is a good idea for our kids to get out of this small town environment and try something new. Still, they offered Jessica nothing less than she deserved, a full-paid scholarship and a place on the college volleyball team.

Jessica was easy to find on the local college campus and happily shared all she knew about the blonde girl who came rushing past her yesterday and whose name, as it turned out, was Amber Tilton.

"I don't know her well, Mrs. Wright," Jessica said. "We don't hang out with the same crowd, if you know what I mean."

I was pretty clear about what she meant. Jessica was not a gossip, but she was telling me what I could surmise on my own, that Amber had gotten mixed up with the wrong people. Just a couple of weekend parties, a few slips into the world of temptation and a kid could ruin his or her reputation and be lost in a place she really didn't want to be in, but was helpless to know how to get out of.

"What grade is she in?" I asked.

"Eleventh, I think, maybe tenth. She has to be in one or the other. We were on the yearbook staff together last year, and she showed such potential I put her in charge of the Freshman Page. I remember she was on the Homecoming Committee, too. She did pretty well in Mr. Bennet's chem class, and she had a good attendance record."

The reference to Mr. Bennet meant she had worked pretty hard academically. He was the hardest teacher at the high school and felt it was his personal duty to make sure the kids were prepared for college. If you failed his class, it almost guaranteed the local college wouldn't even look at you. It was less about subject matter, than about rigor.

The reference to attendance was from Jessica herself who took her school responsibilities seriously. If Amber had a high absentee rate, Jessica would not have entrusted her with duties on the yearbook.

"Is she still at the high school?" I asked.

"Yes ma'am, I think so. She looked awful, Mrs. Wright. Do you think she is in a lot of trouble?"

"Not sure, Jess, but I'll do my best to help her out if she is."

Jessica was unclear about the guy Amber had been with. She didn't recognize the car by description, and a good kid like Jessica would have no idea why anybody would be down that road.

"It doesn't lead anywhere," Jessica said.

No, it didn't, except to a lot of trouble.

****

If you ever visit a high school, you may wonder who the hardest working person is. Having been a teacher, I can tell you that a teacher's job is a lot harder than anybody knows. And the students aren't having a walk in the park either. But if you came to Morton High School, you would never know who the hardest working person is because she makes it look so effortless. That's what masters do. They give a flawless performance, then make you think it was as easy as pie.

Now, personally I've never understood that adage because I've made a pie and it is on my "never do this again" list. It is not easy.

Sandra McCawley smiled at me as I came in the front door. She was on the phone, simultaneously writing a pass for a student, pressing the intercom to a teacher's room and asking a parent what she could do to help. I stepped to the side and watched her hand off the pass, speak into the intercom to let a teacher know a parent was here to meet with him, assure the person on the phone that, yes, graduation was scheduled for May 21st, and motioned me to come forward all in one seamless effort. What a girl!

For better or for worse, I had decided not to tell Billy what I knew about Amber. I thought I might be able to get more out of her if I approached it from the "concerned mom" perspective than the "I'm going to arrest you as an accessory to a crime" perspective. I'd tell Billy after I talked with her, especially if my method proved unfruitful. Did I mean to say fruitful? Okay, I was worried that I would fail Billy again. I had gotten Fred shot, lost the only lead on the case, and still hadn't gotten any closer to finding out why all this had happened.

Once, I accidentally left the gate open at my grandfather's and let his cows out. I was terrified. I nearly killed myself running all over the place herding them back in until I had the brilliant idea they would all come back for dinner. Sure enough, they all came running at the first whiff of corn mush. I figured this would work for Billy, too. Not the corn mush, but the information that would lead to solving the crime. He'd be happy again and maybe I would not be in his doghouse anymore.

I had a cover story all ready for being at the school. The fact that my children attended there would have been grounds enough, but this is why I always get caught when I try to do the wrong thing: I double my efforts to cover up what I am really up to. Not only is my face an ineffectual tool for lying, but also, my cover stories would pass for Russian novels. When one reason would be enough, I give three. That and my breathless recitation of them, makes my listener suspicious.

I am frequently on campus to do stories about students, teachers, events, even school board meetings, and this time I needed to do a story on Jeremy Milligan, a recent scholarship winner. I had called ahead and made an appointment so my turning up was not a clue that something might be up.

"Hi, Sandra," I said when I finally got my turn at the front desk. "I …"

"Yep," she smiled, "Got you set up in the library conference room."

I should have known. As competent as she is, of course she would have everything taken care of.

"And could I get Amber Tilton's schedule? I was going to talk to her about prom." When Sandra looked puzzled, I added, "Jessica Hanover suggested it."

That was the magic word, or words. Sandra printed out the schedule and handed it to me. If I was reading it right, Amber had Yearbook Staff in the library around the time I would be finished with Jeremy. Maybe I could catch her then.

The high school was practically brand new. It had been a hard battle to get it, but the town's people had agreed to an extra tax to fund its construction. It was laid out well, in my opinion, having taught in very old schools and in relatively new ones that looked more like the Taj Mahal than a place of learning. You had to wonder who was supposed to be impressed. The kids really didn't care where they learned as long as it was clean. Teachers were so busy teaching, they hardly had time to look around at their own rooms, much less enjoy architectural grandeur.

The entrance to the high school led visitors straight into the office so their business could be transacted. The next feature was the library, open and airy, with rows and rows of books. It also housed conference rooms for parent-teacher meetings, staff meetings and Special Education Individual

Education Plan meetings.

I went to one of the library conference rooms, but Jeremy wasn't there. I checked the other rooms to make sure he wasn't in those then doubled back to the first conference room and put down my recorder, camera and notebook. He still wasn't there, yet, so I slid the door bar to "Occupied," and turned around to face the books.

Since I like to read, my idea of heaven is time to spare and books on the shelf. I started in the middle of a row and began working my way down the alphabet: Paton, Pasternak, Peck, Poe, …There was one I hadn't read in a while, … I pulled it off the shelf and glanced through the open spot to a face on the other side of the shelf.

It was a familiar face, but it looked wrong somehow. The hair was hanging in strands all over the face. The eyes had telltale dark shadows under them, the kind that meant no sleep, or something else more insidious. The skin was pale and blotchy, uncharacteristic of teen skin that can take lots of abuse from kids who think they will live forever and their skin will, too. I couldn't place that face with its name, but it was one I knew.

Suddenly, the eyes lifted to mine. I never was much for picking out the kids who were on drugs in my classroom. I had to rely on other kids to tell me. All I knew was something wasn't right. Well, this was true of her. Something wasn't right, but what, I couldn't tell you. Her eyes were blue, an unforgettable blue, and then, I remembered. In my mind I had called them Norwegian blue. It was Bretta, the exchange student I had interviewed a few weeks ago. She looked awful, and my stomach was flooded with fear at what had happened to her. I tried to play it off.

"Hi, Bretta" I said in as chipper a voice as I could muster. "How are you?"

This question ranks right up there with stupidest things to say to someone who is in grief, in pain or looks like Bretta did. If I'm such a whiz with words, with my English degrees and being a journalist, what in the world was I doing saying such idiotic things?

Her response was just as generic. "Fine."

Great, monosyllabic responses weren't going to get me very far. Maybe it would help if I coaxed her around the corner so we could see each other face to face instead of through a stack of books.

"Stay right there, I'm coming around."

I moved quickly down the shelves and turned the corner to be on the same row with her. Just then, Jeremy stopped at the end of the same row.

"Hi Mrs. Wright. I'm here."

Now, what was I going to say?

"I'll be right there, hon'; my things are in the first conference room."

That would buy me exactly ten seconds or less to see Bretta and figure out what I could about her condition. Jeremy obediently left. Bretta was just turning around to face me, but as I spoke to Jeremy, she turned back to the book bag she had on the floor instead.

"I must go," she said, in the precise English of one who has learned our language instead of adopting it through conversation.

"Bretta." I said helplessly, and before I could think of anything more to say to her, she was gone. What was I going to do about that?

One of the tenets of my life is from *This Side of Paradise* by F. Scott Fitzgerald. In it, the young protagonist has made a mess of his life and he asks Monsignor Darcy, his mentor, what he should do. "Do the next thing," was his very sage advice. So, even though I was faced with yet another problem I would take on to solve... as if I didn't have enough to solve anyway ... I knew I needed to do the next thing, and that meant going to interview Jeremy.

I tried to be attentive to my interview, though my thoughts wandered back to Bretta. I had my list of questions with a few unique ones so the stories about kids as marvelous as Jeremy didn't all sound the same. Jeremy was a fine boy with a bright future. He was respectful and humorous, just the right combination for a really likable person. We ran through his high school accomplishments and his plans for the future. I interjected some questions like what he saw as the biggest problem in the world he would undertake to resolve.

His answer was provocative. "I don't think I would try to tackle world hunger. That is too big for just one person like me. The best I could do is to help just a few people, and I already do that at the food bank at our church. I want to do something big. I think I'd like to start an exchange program for people to learn about jobs they want to do. Kind of like a mentor program, but with people actually getting the experience in high school that would count as high school credit. I think most kids don't have a clue where to start. Adults always tell us they want us to succeed, but they don't tell us how."

Interesting. You can learn a lot by talking to kids.

I was sure he was going to go far. But what about Bretta? What about Amber? What about dinner? Oh no. I had forgotten about my very own children.

Chapter 14

Since I had Amber's schedule, and she hadn't shown up in the library, but looking for her was going to stir up questions, and I wasn't supposed to be interviewing her anyway, I decided I would redeem myself by going to the store and filling the empty coffers of the Wright pantry.

These days I am doing the hit-or-miss version of grocery shopping. I should make a list like a normal person, then dedicate three hours to the shopping task and just get it done, the right way. Instead, I find myself running in, grabbing things off the shelf like some bandit in a bank-robbing scheme, and racing to the check out line in record time. At least my own flesh and blood would not think I had forgotten them, which I most certainly had.

I stopped back by the office and typed up my story on Jeremy. It was nearly 2:30, and I had an idea. My children would die if I picked them up from school now that they were in high school, but there is no law against a parent being in the parking lot. I could talk to Amber there. I knew plenty of kids who would direct me to her, thus saving my children from the embarrassment of talking to their mother in front of other teenagers, and me from the scolding I was going to get from Elizabeth when she realized I was playing amateur detective, again.

The dual enrollment kids, the ones who were taking

classes at the local college while still being enrolled in high school, had already left and that gave me a place to park in the student parking section. The last bell chimed and the kids started pouring out of the high school like syrup over pancakes. Marcus Bryant was the nearest to me.

"Hi, Mrs. Wright. Do you want Elizabeth or Emily?"

"No, honey, I was actually looking for Amber Tilton. I needed to ask her about prom."

When I was a teacher, I could tell when a kid had something to say. Clearly, Marcus had a response to what I was telling him. The question was, could I get him to say it?

"Is there something wrong, Marcus?"

He hesitated.

"Marcus, you know I have Amber's best interest at heart"

He relented.

"I don't think Amber can help you, Mrs. Wright. She hasn't been on the prom committee for a long time. In fact, she usually isn't even at school."

"Was she absent today?"

"No ma'am, she skipped. She does that a lot."

"It sounds like this girl is in trouble."

"She is Mrs. Wright, but the kind of trouble she wants to be in. We've all tried to talk to her. She won't listen. She hangs out with the townies and the dropouts."

To the untrained ear, those two descriptors mean nothing, but to me, they were informative. In our college town, there is a clear division in the ranks of the high school age kids.

On one side are those who are going to go on to college or who get a high school diploma and take their place in their little community with jobs or businesses. But, on the other side, are those who just get their diploma, but never do anything further to contribute to society. At the end of that same spectrum are those who "drop out" of high school altogether. This group comprised those Marcus referred to as the "townies and dropouts."

There would be absolutely nothing wrong with not finishing high school if the kids who chose that route invested in something else, like a trade or honest labor, like the kids who took up their parent's businesses or started one of their own, thereby becoming a member of their little community, making it stronger with employment and being a tax-paying citizen.

Instead, the townies and the dropouts just drifted from one hangout to another after being run off by the local police when the citizenry got fed up with their drug use, loud music and abusive behavior.

Because this lifestyle is so appealing to the teen mind that rebels against doing what is required to provide for a future that appears elusive, that group of adolescents, the townies, were joined by the kids who were disenchanted with school, swelling their ranks with the dour, the resistant and the profane. I can't think of anything more painful than seeing a kid after a couple of years in this lifestyle, having witnessed them in the fresh spring of youth with lots of potential.

Typically, they are strung out on drugs, their youth

stolen by the aging process of decadence. They don't eat well, and although most teens don't, the unmistakable signs of malnourishment are written in the deep pockets under their eyes and the lines riddled on their faces.

It is a desperate thing to see, like a child drowning just outside your arm's reach. Though my heart aches for them, once they start down this path, the only thing that will save them is themselves. I can't, though I have tried. The same self-determination that would keep them from slipping down this slope would bring them back. It can't be taught; it comes from somewhere within.

If Marcus was right, Amber was probably too far-gone. Maybe I couldn't bring her back from the land of the Lotus-Eaters, but I could give her the chance to do the right thing by turning in the boy who had shot Fred.

"Where are they these days?"

But Marcus was shaking his head. "Mrs. Wright, I don't think you should try to find her. It is really too dangerous for you."

I wanted to say I was an adult and had nothing to fear from a group of kids. When fights broke out in my classroom, I had no compunction about getting in the middle of them because I knew the combatants would break it up rather than see me hurt. But in this case, Marcus was right. These kids were rogues, with no sense of respect for authority or adults, much less any sense of me. I would be seen as an intruder, an enemy. Marcus was warning me, and because I am heedless, I asked:

"Where?"

"The Corn Dog," he quietly replied.

Chapter 15

If you go into an old building, even though she is aging, you may see she is still a grand lady with opulent lighting fixtures, carved wood molding, extravagant draperies, a hint of the ancient glory. Maybe she is not a dowager, but a lady of poetry and hard living; she has character and dignity. But there are other buildings that should just be torn down. They have no sense of themselves, no story in their paneling, just the deterioration of years gone by ravaging her beyond her usefulness.

The Corn Dog was one of those buildings. It sat on the edge of a huge ravine, so if it didn't topple over on its own, a bulldozer push in the right spot could have eased the eyesore into its welcome grave.

When the highway was the only thoroughfare between the two large cities on either side of Morton, The Corn Dog was a popular stop. It served cold drinks, fries and, of course, the self-reputed "Best Corn Dog in the World." Once the interstate went in, this section of the highway was frequented only by locals who knew better than to believe the now-faded signs of false advertising. It wasn't long before only the kids ate there because they could afford the $1.25 corn dog and fifty-five cent drink and free refills.

It is always sad to watch the death of a thing, how age and gravity pull and tug at it until there is nothing left of life.

I always avoided that section of the highway because it reminded me too much of watching my parents die. I should have avoided it today, but I can't help myself. Once I start something, I have to finish it, even if it finishes me.

From the looks of the kids and the cars in the parking lot, that is exactly what was going to happen. They were smoking and leaning on the car hoods, not so different from the young hooligans in *Rebel without a Cause*. The girls wore sleazy outfits with the obvious intent of seducing their companions, and I wondered why they would want to attract the boys who were there. They could have all used a bath and could have made a hundred bucks posing for the next detergent commercial.

"Look what our soap can get out!" I heard the announcer say in my head.

I decided to stay in my car and simply roll up near them, speaking out my car window to them.

"Hi, I was looking for Amber Tilton," I said as unparentlike as I could to the crowd of reprobates.

"Why?" a harsh-looking girl asked haughtily.

"Well, I…"

"We don't know nobody named Amber," a particularly tall and swarthy fellow said as he began to walk toward my car.

As if on cue, several of the boys broke from the crowd and began to circle my car. For a desperate moment, I realized I should press the gas pedal and race away, but my innate sense of child protection kept me from doing that. If I hit one of them, I would never forgive myself. It didn't occur to me they probably would have had the good sense to get out of my way. Without my realizing it, one of them had come up on my left. Quick as a snake, his hand reached in and jerked my keys out of the ignition.

"Hey, give me those!" I yelled, in spite of my precariously unsafe position.

He jangled the keys in front of my face, then snatched them away as I reached for them. Another boy reached in the open window and opened the door, proof that locked doors only work if the window is closed. I wondered if he was going to drag me out.

"S'pose you tell us what yer doin' here."

"I'm just looking for Amber."

Several of them spoke at once.

"You a social worker?"

"Her mom?"

"The law?"

"No," I said in as steady a voice as I could manage. "I just want to make sure she is safe."

For some reason, they thought that was funny. The boy slammed the door he had just opened. I was relieved, but I shouldn't have been. The boys decided another funny thing would be to get on the bumpers of my car and bounce up and down. I wasn't sure if I would be safer in the car or out. Two of them who looked like they were on something, and given my inability to figure that out should have told me how obvious it was, got on the right side of the car and started pushing the roof. My little car was no match for their adolescent strength and, despite being a metal vehicle, gave in easily to them shoving and rocking it from front to back.

"Quit that," I yelled.

"Hey J.D., le's see if we can turn it over," one of them said.

Suddenly, the two boys were joined by four more. Now, instead of bouncing back and forth, I was rocking from side to side, dangerous in itself, but even more so because of my proximity to the ravine. The car was going to go over. Some of the girls had joined in chanting, "Toss it, toss it," and were crowding around to encourage the boys. I was in serious trouble and fumbled for my purse. The jolting made me pull at it too fast and everything in it tumbled into the floor.

"Maybe I should try to get out," I thought, but then, I'd be at their mercy.

The squeal of tires from another part of the parking lot attracted their attention. It was an old Chevrolet with lots of seat room and the seats were all filled up. Nothing about the inhabitants of the new car made me feel any better. They were more kids, and from the looks of them, they were the same breed of animal. For the time being, the attack on my car stopped, but I was helpless to escape because one of the reprobates still had my keys.

Two other similar modeled cars pulled in behind the Chevrolet. Several of the occupants got out and spoke to the gang from The Corn Dog. They exchanged the usual fist smacks, thumb handshakes and shoulder bumps of the "cool" kids.

"Whas up, muchacho?"

"Hey Dude."

"Whatcha you got here, man?"

"Some nosey ..."

"Yo, Dude, not cool."

I was too stunned to recognize the voice of someone who was going to be my savior. I had been watching the exchange between what appeared to be the two gang leaders, realizing I had stumbled into a drug buy. No wonder they were so hostile. They had everything to lose by my being here, and nothing to lose by my being gone.

With a wave of his hand, the newest gang leader motioned the boys away from my car.

"Yo, Ms. Wright, whatcha doin' here? This is no place for a lady," he said.

Did my face show the relief I felt?

"Oh, Jorge," was all I could manage to say. I pronounced his name in the old, familiar "George" of our time together in my classroom. He had been embarrassed to be the only Hispanic in class and wanted to fit in, so he'd insisted I called him the Anglicized "George" rather than pronouncing it in the vernacular of his native tongue, "Hor-hey."

My mind briefly went back in time. One day I had brought sundaes for the class because he suggested it, and to make him the hero to his peers. It worked. He was their champion, who had convinced the teacher to bring ice cream; he was a favorite student of mine, too, at once respectful and endearing.

But the lure of the easy road was too powerful to overcome, and those four precious years in high school that seem like four dog years to a teenager, proved too long to invest. Jorge had dropped out. Sometimes students who drop out come back for a visit, but Jorge was not one of them.

Bringing me back to the present, recalling the last time I saw him, I heard him say, "Really, Ms. Wright, you should go."

The other leader grabbed him by the shoulder.

"You crazy, man? Let her go? No way."

Jorge grabbed the other boy's hand and though I could not see the grasp clearly, the boy's face contorted with pain; I knew Jorge had squeezed it tightly.

"She should go," Jorge said to the other leader with a force I had never heard from him. To me, he said, "Hey, Ms. Wright, you'll go, won't you?"

"Yes, Jorge, just as soon as someone gives me my keys." I looked into the crowd.

Jorge didn't say anything, just held out his hand to the group of boys standing around him. One of them stepped forward and handed him my keys. Jorge turned, smiled and handed them to me. As he did, I could not miss the unmistakable "13" tattooed on the web between his thumb and forefinger.

I'd been out of the classroom for a while, but I knew what that tattoo meant. It, along with other of the gang's symbols, had started showing up in the graffiti at the school where I taught. We had a specially called faculty meeting to alert us about things to watch out for.

"Don't confront the gang members openly," the vice principal had said. "This gang is treacherous and has no qualms about the violence they use. If you suspect gang involvement, let me know. We'll need to keep a roster of gang membership in our student body."

When one of my students had told me he suspected Jorge of falling into the gang life, I wasn't sure what to do. But one morning as I entered the front lobby, Jorge was standing at the end of the hall. I felt compelled to walk right up to him and ask him. Instead, I put my arms around him, and the tears began to pour.

Jorge was so quiet. "Don't cry Mrs. Wright. It will be alright."

"No, it won't Jorge," I sobbed. "They are going to kill you."

It wasn't much later when I no longer saw him at school. I knew what had happened. He had slipped away from me into the life of a gang member. Now, here he was again, but this was not the reunion I had anticipated.

He smiled down at me sitting in my car.

"Jorge," I said softly, the tears welling up in my eyes.

"You should go now, Ms. Wright. Okay? Yes, go now."

I knew that Jorge had saved my life. I wish I could say I had done the same for him.

Chapter 16

If I had a hat, I would have held it in my hands when I went to see Billy. If there were such a thing as humble fruit, I would have made a big pie and eaten the whole thing myself after he finished with me. Clearly, I had been in over my head, and Providence had smiled on my naïveté and ignorance, preserving my life. Laughed heartily, more like.

Billy's thundercloud of a face told me just how much trouble I was in, standing before his desk after my confession. He let fly.

"Where do I start? Withholding vital information of an attempted murder investigation after endangering Fred's life? Trying to track down a suspect on your own and withholding that information, too. You endangered your own life, and at the very least, you're a victim of aggravated assault, but now you refuse to file charges on one of the aggressors because you don't want to involve an ex-student?

"You got into the midst of drug activity and nearly destroyed years of undercover work for the infiltration of '13.' Does that about sum it up?

"The Drug Enforcement Agency officer who is working on this case wants me to hand you over for prosecution, and I already have a hard time keeping the local people from hauling you off to jail for the meddling you do. It was bad enough that Fred's family was mad at you. I should never have let you get started on that van. I've turned you into a vigilante who thinks she knows more than the professionals around her."

I learned that when a man is on a rant, to just let him get it out. I stood quietly wincing with every verbal slash of wrongdoing he swiped at me. Just when I thought he was finished, he delivered the mother of all blows. And he said it softly, which is far more powerful than any added volume can create.

"To say nothing of the trust I had in you."

"Had?"

Had.

Past tense. As an ex-English teacher, I knew what past tense meant.

Ouch.

I don't think he could have said anything harsher. Let's see. Ten years in prison. Being fired from your journalism job. Life without parole. Oh wait. He could have said, like my dad did once when I had acted up in public: "I'm so disappointed in you."

Yeah, that one from my dad did it.

Nope. For Billy, the "had" worked just fine. It was the worst thing he could have said to me. Worse still, he wouldn't look at me. He just sat at his desk shaking his head.

I didn't even try the, "Yeah, but I…" defense. Yeah, but I got the name of the girl in the car with the guy who shot Fred. Yeah, but I found out who was filtering drugs into our town. Yeah, but I'm not dead. I was pretty sure Billy would have been all right if I had been.

I opened my mouth with some form of contrition:

Would "I'm sorry?" work? ...oooh, such a paltry phrase.

How about "I was only trying to help?" yech, sounded stupid even to me.

No, there was nothing left to say.

I don't think I walked out of his office; I crawled on my belly in shame. Only one thing was going to fix this. I needed some John Wayne. After a day like this, I needed all the good old American spirit of the fight I could muster.

I'd been in love with The Duke since I was a teenager While the rest of my pack was in love with the latest teen pop idol. the classic movie icons: Clark Gable, Paul Newman, Robert Mitchum, Yul Brynner and, of course, John Wayne, were my kind of men.

It wasn't until I found myself sobbing through *Rio Grande* as a grown-up woman that I realized what I loved about John Wayne...his strength. It made me think of my daddy, the tower of strength in my life. Why watching John Wayne gave me comfort is a mystery for the psychiatrists who are brave enough to take on the maniacal workings of my mind to figure out. It was just a movie. He was portraying a character that didn't really exist. John Wayne, like my daddy, was dead, but watching him in action gave me what I needed to go on.

When I'm feeling shaken by the world, scared by events, overwhelmed by my duties as only parent to my brood, I pop in a John Wayne movie and feel his strength. If I have a task I have to power through, and I'm weary, wanting to give up, I'll pop in George C. Scott's *Patton*. The music alone helps me finish that paint job, construct that garden bower, vacuum that rug.

If it's creativity I need, I'll listen to jazz or classical music, but no amount of creativity was going to get me out of this mess. I needed some strength. So tonight, it was going to be *True Grit*, and I was Baby Sister, Maddie. John was going to save me from the villain Ned Pepper, and the rattlesnakes and even the rattlesnake bite.

The drive home was a long one. When I am alone, I talk to myself, reasoning out things that have happened. Sometimes, I will even role-play and act out my reactions to things to see if they are logical.

But, even *I* couldn't stand myself right now. I didn't want to hear my inane voice, or my inadequate excuses, or my hollow justifications.

I had been nothing but a miserable failure. I hadn't found Amber. I hadn't found her accomplice who shot Fred. I hadn't found out what was wrong with Bretta. I hadn't cooked dinner for my children.

I was going to have to do penance. I was going to do that story on Garth Miller; I was going to make a homemade dinner for my kids, not drive-through; I was going to apologize every day to Billy; I was going to stop being so overly curious.

I had found Jorge, but only to lose him again. I could see him lying dead in a gang related killing, and it made me cry. When I had taught him, he was such a sweet, gentle boy, uneasy in the new world of public school and English-speaking peers.

Gangs seduced our youth with promises of family-like loyalty and easy money, then played them like pawns for their own purposes. Young boys, in a search for manhood found the power of strength from other males and the cold steel of a gun in their hand irresistible. Jorge would not likely see his 25th birthday, maybe even less for having stepped in to save my life.

I hadn't solved a single problem, and I had created dozens more.

The kids knew something was up when I walked in the door. Although I should have spilled my guts about the whole mess, I couldn't take seeing Elizabeth standing in the doorway, tapping her little foot and pronouncing those hateful, ugly words...

"I told you so."

Surely, no one in the whole human race could believe that those words would ever help. They say them simply to validate interference in your business. They say them to be smug and self-righteous. They say them to justify the existence of mankind, but they don't say them to make you feel better.

In this case, she would have said them because she is truly concerned that I get in over my head, and she was right. She was and I do.

Dinner was ready, a lovely casserole with a crisp spinach and endive salad, crunchy French bread and lots of dressing choices, but the thought of food made me want to cry; a strange reaction, but in keeping with my mood. After all, I didn't deserve such wonderful children who made dinner for me when I was supposed to have done that for them.

When I headed straight for the television, plucked John Wayne out of the DVD stack, flopped on the couch and sighed, the girls knew things were very bad. It wasn't long before Emily handed me a bowl of moose tracks ice cream, a sure cure for what ails you, unless it is the reason you are on the couch, because you ate too much of it, in which case, it *is* what ails you.

We were all curled up together each in our special niches in the living room couches, when the outside world invaded our peace.

****

Even though I have an answering machine, if the phone rings, I will still kill myself trying to answer it. I'm not sure if that means I am a responsible adult who believes in talking to the people who want to talk to me, or part of another obsessive-compulsive behavior that I ought to be investigating instead of parked cars in various parts of our town.

I answered on the third ring, having fallen off the couch trying to reach for the remote, stubbing my toe on the coffee table, and tripping over one of the dogs lounging on the floor. If there was an Olympic category for overcoming obstacles to answer the phone, I could enter it and take the gold, handily.

It was Steve.

"You don't have to do the Garth Miller story," he said.

I thought the next two words out of his mouth were going to be: "You're fired."

Instead, they were:

"He's dead."

Chapter 17

"Dead?"

"Yep. Found him in the back of his BMW, hood over his head. Glock bullet in the mess of what's left of him."

Execution style.

"You need me to come in?"

"No. I got it. Just wanted to tell you about it."

I wasn't sure if Billy would even talk to me ever again, so, of course, Steve would handle Garth's murder story himself. Word travels fast in this town like it does in all small towns, so I was pretty sure Steve was aware of my current *persona non-grata* status at the sheriff's department. Even though I wasn't sure where Garth's body had been found, and whose jurisdiction it was anyway, I have always been *persona non-grata* at our city police department, my present misbehavior notwithstanding, so they certainly wouldn't be sharing information with me. Steve stood a far better chance of getting it. I was trying to be generous, even though I didn't feel it.

"Sounds like a great story." I was going to push for some details.

"Yeah, it feels good to get the old investigative reporting juices flowing again.""Where was he found? City Hall parking lot?" I figured Garth would come to his end inside his dominion.

"Uh-uh. And here's the strange thing. They found him, I should say found his car, with him in the trunk, parked on your interstate ramp. Same place you found that van a couple of weeks ago. What do you think that's all about?"

Darn it! Great story, right here in my own back yard and I couldn't touch it because I had been...what did Billy call me... Oh yeah, a vigilante.

And it sounded like Steve was pumping *me* for information for *his* story.

Double Darn!

If I had behaved myself, I would be the one doing this story. I'd be trailing behind Billy's guys, following every move. I'd be in on the investigation, getting an exclusive.

Then, I did something I am not proud of. I decided to turn the tables on Steve. I knew he was hungry for the story, and I could feed that hunger while getting the information I wanted. I was still a good journalist, and I still wanted to do this story. It was one of the hottest we had seen, and I didn't want to miss out on that. I could get Steve to get information I couldn't get on my own.

I massaged my conscience about what I was about to do by reminding myself that Steve would be getting a great story for his sweetheart, *The World,* and I would be eliminating crime in my little town, perhaps also reinstating myself in the journalistic loop.

"Wow, Steve. That is incredible. So, they found his body? Who?"

"Now, that's the strange thing. It was a city policeman who found it."

"What?"

"Yeah, isn't that strange? Weren't we just looking at the problem that the city police weren't even patrolling the city streets they do have jurisdiction over? What was one of *their* guys doing out your way? That's Billy's turf, and the interstate belongs to the troopers. You think they were visiting down one of your dirt roads and that was why they were out that way?"

"Who was it?" I asked, hoping Steve had already gleaned that piece of information.

"Don't know, but I'm going to find out. You think they found out about Tyner's spot?"

Steve was remembering when I uncovered a lover's lane out this way, and who should be in it, but Bruce Tyner. No, I didn't think that. To my knowledge, the city police had not availed themselves of the convenient trysting locale down my road. And most of the rags who were on Billy's payroll were now going over the county line to a hotel for their romantic rendezvous; at least they had the decency to buy the girl a room.

Bruce's girl had to content herself with a backseat for comfort, in a police cruiser no less. Maybe Bruce was afraid his capabilities in the bedroom area warranted him keeping her prisoner.

Oh, that was ugly wasn't it? I was in no position to be mean to anyone.

"No, I don't think it was Tyner's spot," I said. "He's one of Billy's guys, so his presence wouldn't arouse suspicion if seen out here on the road. You said it was a city policeman.

Now one of their cruisers would be unusual. *They* were out this way? Hmmm. You think they *knew* Garth would be there?"

"Why?"

"You aren't going to like this answer. I think the reason why a city policeman knew that Garth would be found there is because he had been told he would."

"You mean, someone *told them* where to find his body?"

"Yep."

"Who?"

"Well, Steve, that would be the million dollar question you need to ask."

"I don't think they are going to answer it."

"You know something, Steve, I have learned everything I know from you."

I hoped at this moment I had so dazed him with flattery that he would not be thinking about the huge mess I had just made and think I was giving him credit for THAT. I continued in case he did.

"I can get people to tell me things they don't think they know, and things they don't want to tell me. I learned that from you. You need to get yourself over to the city police department and have a talk with the guy who reported Garth's car. Tell him you want to do a feature on the way law enforcement is doing such a great job. Tell him you are so impressed with his discovery, you are sure that he should be up for a promotion."

My instructions to Steve had a two-fold purpose. On the

one hand, men do not flatter each other easily, especially an old curmudgeon like Steve. I was feeding him lines I knew he would not otherwise think of, and given our relationship with the city police, Steve's usual methods of intimidation weren't going to gain much. No, flattery was going to have to do it. And Steve needed coaching in that area.

The second reason I was instructing him was because I would never get within a football field of the city police department before they shut down the lines of communication, and there was information I needed. Steve didn't have anyone else to talk to about this story. He was going to call me back and share everything he had found out with me. I needed that information because I had a hunch I knew who had killed Garth, and I thought I knew why. If I was right, I also knew what had happened to Delago Fuentez.

"Okay Mib. I'll let you know what I find out. Oh, and Mib? Sorry about the other thing. I've got some feature stories for you to pick up. Your byline will not suffer."

I knew Steve was just trying to be nice, but it is a comedown to do nothing but features when you have been used to following in the fray. He wasn't gloating. He's not like that. And the reference to the byline meant he wasn't cutting the number of stories I did for our paper just because I was out of favor.

But that was all for tomorrow morning, and if I played my cards right, I was not going to be doing those stories after all. I was going to be front page all the way. The first thing I needed to do was get my camera out and have a look at those pictures I had taken of Delago's (or should I say Marvella's) van the day I found it.

I kept all my digital pictures in duplicate on my computer. I have never trusted technology, and more times than I'd like to remember, I was right not to. If your livelihood depends on the use of technology, nothing will give you a heart attack faster than the loss of your information. In the early days of the computer, "Backup your data!" was the user's mantra; it is still true today.

I scrolled through the set of pictures from that story. Cigarette butts. Side view of the van. Back view of the van. Inside the van. Not there. But I knew something had to be. There would be no sleeping tonight. These pictures and I were going to get very well acquainted. I started looking for my magnifying glass. And when I was finished with the pictures, I was headed to the office.

****

When I was a teacher, I kept folders for each of the curriculum items I taught. If it was a unit, there would be multiple folders all color-coded and in the order they would be taught. I took that strategy with me when I came to the newspaper business, and tonight it would pay off.

I liked to go to the office after hours. It was so quiet and peaceful with no clackety-clack of the computer keyboard, no bbbrrriiing of the telephone or Steve's yelling or Gladys's droning voice taking messages and dealing with customers or The Sports Guy complaining about all the work he did and not getting paid for it.

When I fitted the key into the back door of the office, it was 7:00 P.M. I hadn't pulled an all-nighter in a long time, but I was pretty sure I was going to need copious amounts of caffeine. I brewed a pot of coffee while I went to my filing cabinet.

If I did a story on an environmental issue, I did the background research for my facts, then kept the notes in a labeled folder in my cabinet. I kept my journalist notebooks right side up in order of date. That wasn't going to help me because I wasn't sure of the dates I needed. One promising thing, though, was that I had put all the story contents in order on the front covers of the notebooks. That meant a quick scan of the front cover would tell me if I needed to look in it.

I started with the earliest notebook. Since I wasn't sure how far back to start, it seemed logical to begin with the most recent story and work backwards through the timeline. That included the city council meeting just this past week. Had there been anything there? Zoning. What was being zoned? Oh yeah, the city's relatively new industrial park. It was in Billy's zone for patrol and the city police chief was asking for a rezoning so it would be under his jurisdiction. Why?

I started digging for the industrial park story. Who owned property there? What was their business? I started with the thread of it and was on my third cup of coffee when my cell phone rang at 10:30.

"Hey Mibbie, did I wake you?" It was Steve.

"No," I said, trying to sound as sleepy as I was pretending to be. I knew Steve would come down to the office, if he knew where I was, but I was certain I could get more done without any interference from him.

"I got hold of the city policeman who took the call. He comes on duty at 11:00. I'm going to meet with him after the duty roster is called, and see what I can find out."

"Fabulous, Steve. I can't wait to hear what he says."

"You want me to call you after I talk to him? It'll be late."

"No, that's alright. We can talk in the morning. I'll come in early and you can fill me in. Do you need any background information for your story?"

"Well, I guess there's the usual: when Garth got elected; family connections; his civic work."

"Okay, I'll dig it up for you."

"Thanks, Mibs, you're a champ."

Steve disconnected, and I turned back to the notes I had been studying. I was going to have to hurry, so Steve wouldn't see the office light on when he went to the police station. It looked like the industrial park was divided into parcels, but it had been owned, originally, by just one man: Harvey Layfield, our local car dealer.

Chapter 18

Harvey had had an idea to open a new car lot alongside the interstate to attract attention to his stock of cars, but in the end, he'd decided to stick with his old dealership and his illegal gambling machines in the garage. He had sold the property to ...who? Garth Miller and his friend Senator Barney Hughes! Oh my!

Now, I remembered. Senator Hughes had used his state influence to pull in some pork barrel spending on the roads around the industrial park to make it more accessible and attractive. When that wasn't enough, he had backed the project with his own money. Where was Garth in all of this?

I pulled out my notes on the industrial park. It was such a laudable name: "Morton Industrial Park." There were really only trucking companies there. I wasn't sure if that counted as industrial, but at least there was something to show for all that money. How much had passed hands?

Then I remembered some gossip I had picked up, when was it, a year ago? Some thug-types had made their way around town, and as with every stranger, or two, they had attracted a lot of attention. Was that when I had seen Garth with some new faces?

Billy had asked them point-blank what their business was and they had told him they were visiting a friend from here: Harvey Layfield. Harvey had attracted attention of his own with a new house, new truck and frequent trips out of town. Most people thought it was because of all the money he had made off the sale of the land.

I fingered the telephone keypad of my desk phone. It was almost 11:00, and I would be disturbing the Layfield home if I made the phone call I contemplated. Not to mention that at any minute, Steve would be cruising up to the city police department. On the other hand, it was entirely possible that Harvey Layfield was having a late night of his own. I grabbed my purse and headed out the door for The Blue Moon.

Chapter 18

My tires crunched on the gravel in the parking lot, and I cringed with each sound. I don't know why I thought I could creep into a public place, but I wanted to. Only the worst of our town's disreputable people went to the Blue Moon, and here I was in their company. Even when I was young and impetuous, I wouldn't have come here.

When I made my rounds to the local law enforcement agencies for the latest arrest records each week to post in the news, The Blue Moon patrons always made the list. There was the usual weekend drunken brawl, the lover's or marital spat, the guy who drank too much and came out swinging when they tried to wake him up after closing time, and the someone, male or female, who was too drunk to call a cab, and decided to drive home instead, thus landing him or her with a DUI.

I heaved all of my self-confidence up onto my shoulders and got out of the car. With each step toward the door, I had horrible thoughts. What if I met my second grade teacher coming out of the bar? How would I explain myself? Of course logically, my second grade teacher couldn't be coming out of the bar, I was pretty sure she was already dead. And if I had been at all lucid, I would have realized that if she were coming out, she could have no words of condemnation as I was going in. But my mind was humming from lack of sleep and too much caffeine, so I wasn't making much sense, not even to me.

The lights from the blinking sign above were eerie and yellow, stretching seductively across the path leading up to the big blue door. On it, was painted a round circle that I am sure the artist meant to be a moon. The clientele were not so discriminating that they complained his rendering didn't match reality. I put my trembling hand on the metal knob, trying not to think of the other hands that had touched it and where they had been. Surely someone had had the decency to spill a drink on it and kill the germs with the alcohol.

I'd heard about this phenomenon, of being momentarily blinded by darkness, which I certainly was when I finally heaved the monstrous door open. I'd also heard that they keep the lights low in a place like this, so you aren't sure whom you are going home with, until it is too late. I stood still while my eyes adjusted to my surroundings.

There was a girl up on a makeshift stage singing into a karaoke mike about how she "keyed" her boyfriend's car and he was going to find out later. I wanted to point out that while carving up leather seats and taking a baseball bat to headlights sounded like a good way to take revenge on a lover's lack of monogamy, it would certainly land her in jail along with a hefty fine for her destruction of personal property. She actually looked too intoxicated to have been able to do much of anything, and I wasn't here to argue with her.

I wondered at the protocol. Should I wait to be seated, or take a seat at the closest place? Would my vision improve so I could scan the bar? Was the best vista of the room from the bar or a table? While I debated these burning questions, one of the less steady customers made his way swerving toward me. He smelled like a Budweiser factory, and slurred his speech so thoroughly I couldn't quite make out what he said.

Was it: "Toad Nancy?" or "Like Snampsy?" I tried the polite response, no matter what it was.

"No. Thank you."

"Ah, c'mon." And my new admirer grabbed my arm.

I have always been attractive to drunken men and especially to stinking drunk men, so I was not entirely out of my element. Since he was trying to lead me to the dance floor, I surmised he had asked me to dance with him. However, I was also pretty sure the only dance we would have been able to do together was the Mexican hat dance where he passed out on the floor and I danced around him.

This time, I didn't just politely decline, I sprinted in between tables, sure that he would be caught by various chair legs and table edges that would keep him from pursuing me.

My admirer was stalled, so I took the opportunity to look for a less obvious place to wait for my vision to return. I took a seat at a table, near the unhappy singer on the stage, and hidden in a dark corner. It wasn't long before I was accosted by a waitress dressed in a low-cut shirt and tight jeans.

She meant business, and I knew enough of bar practice that you are not allowed to stay unless you get a drink. I also knew not to ask for just plain water, because she would probably charge me seven dollars for it and if I struck her wrong, she might spit in it. I asked for a Miller-Lite. I hoped that was on the menu. She seemed pacified with my choice, and went on her way.

I had been so mortified at having to come here, I didn't think to look for Harvey's unmistakable new truck in the parking lot. I was in luck. Since it was a weeknight, only the most avid drunkards were here.

Two men sat hunched over their drinks at the bar. They were so attentive to their glasses you would have thought they were gazing into Narcissus's pool.

Another very intoxicated man sat over at a table and fought with the waitress every time she tried to take the empties. He was making a collection of them in front of him; I counted ten from where I sat.

A couple, also heavily intoxicated, was arguing ferociously. Though their conversation was loud. I couldn't make out what they were saying. Slurred speech was probably the culprit. The waitress slammed my beer on the table, jarring me out of my interior scan.

"Five bucks," she said, with no fondness in her voice, for her job, her life or me in general. Either she was kin to Gussie, from The Inn, or there was a conspiracy among the waitresses in this town to give the worst service possible.

I didn't argue, I just reached in my purse and pulled out

the money. I guess she knew I wasn't going to be running a tab, and she probably realized she wasn't going to get a tip. I figured the five bucks would cover whatever her service had been worth, so I didn't feel too bad about not supporting this working girl. I resumed my search for Harvey as she disappeared into the darkness.

Someone was over in the far corner of the bar, just enough out of sight that I couldn't make out if it was a male or a female. I decided that I should try to pass casually by, but that was going to be difficult. How did one "pass by" a corner?

The good thing about alcoholics is they are so self-absorbed, they don't take much notice of anything else. I slipped away from my table and headed for the corner. By now my eyesight had returned, so I wasn't bumping table corners with my hip bone, a very painful occurrence indeed.

I recognized Harvey from the many billboards of his face he had set up all over town. Since he was the only dealership in our area, it had seemed superfluous for him to waste his money on advertising. He must have liked the sight of himself 400 times his normal size.

"Hey, Harvey," I said as I slid into the chair across from him. "How are you?"

His head toggled from one side to the other as he raised his eyes to mine.

"D'I know you?" he managed to schlep out.

"Yeah, Mibbie Wright. Gee, Harvey, you remember me don't you?" I tried to sound hurt that our close acquaintanceship was not uppermost in his mind.

"Yeah, I … uh. Yeah, I know you fine. Wanta beer or somethin'?"

"No, thanks, have one." I held up my beer in case he needed proof. "But listen, I was just worried about you, you know?"

"Wha for?"

"Well, you heard about Garth, right?"

His head jerked up and focused in hard on my face. The alcohol content of his brain made it hard to do that.

"Ya know 'bout that?"

"Just me and a couple of other people. Don't worry; I'm not going to tell anybody. I just wanted to check on you and see how you were. After all, no one has figured out yet that you and Garth were business partners. I'm the only one that knows. But, Harvey, someone was very mad at Garth. Do you know why?"

"No. No. No."

One "no" would have been sufficient. He knew.

"Harvey, does anyone know how much Garth gave you for that industrial park land?"

"No."

"But it was more than the million quoted, wasn't it?"

"No."

"Now, look Harvey, it will not take people very long to put this math equation together. You know that Garth was in over his head. Just like you have been in the past. You remember when those Vegas guys came looking for you? Didn't we stand behind you and tell them that we take care of our own? Didn't we protect you from those thugs? We can do that again, Harvey, but you're going to have to help us out."

Billy wouldn't have appreciated being linked with me right now, but hopefully the end would justify the means.

"Cut his tongue out." Harvey took a deep swig of his drink. Not surprisingly, it was stronger than beer. Even though I am not a drinking woman, if I'd been in Harvey's situation, I would have been an expert overnight.

"Yes, they did. These are bad people, not the kind you can play with. How much did Garth pay you for the land?"

"Two five"

"Two thousand five hundred?"

"No, million."

"Harvey, that land is not worth that much."

"And trucks."

"He paid you for trucks?"

"Yeah. M' dealership sells 'em"

The waitress made her way over to us.

"You've got time for another round," she said. "You want one?"

"Yeah," Harvey said.

"No," I said.

The waitress started to walk away to get Harvey another one.

"No," I said loudly. She turned around.

"I heard you," she said tersely.

"No, for him, too," I turned back to him. "Harvey, we've got to get out of here."

"Jus' one more," he said.

"No. I'll get your liquor for you. You can't stay here and you know it."

"Hey, what are you tryin' to pull here," the waitress said. "He can have another drink if he wants it. Who are you to tell him he can't?"

I wasn't sure if this was a proprietary issue over Harvey or the big tip she was expecting from a very drunk customer. Harvey had just started to talk, and I wasn't sure who might come looking for him. I needed him to give me at least a little more information. I reached in my purse and pulled out three twenties.

"Will this cover his?"

"Wait a minute."

"Will it, because if not, I can pull out some more. You want to be paid, but he shouldn't have any more. You know it is illegal to serve a patron more alcohol when he has imbibed too much. This man is clearly intoxicated, and it could be to his detriment to ingest any more. "

I threw in the big vocabulary words as a scare tactic. It usually worked. I was hoping she wouldn't remember that she was in the city police jurisdiction and I would lose this battle with them.

"Okay, whatever. Get him out of here."

I stood up and stepped to Harvey's side of the table. I was hoping he wasn't so far gone he would topple over. I was not strong enough to haul him out, and I wasn't going to be getting any help from in here.

"Come on Harvey. Let's get out of here and get a bottle of your own." Ah, the magic works to a drunk: "more" and "your own" no need to share. Harvey staggered and swayed his way to the front door with me holding on to his arm. I took him straight to my car. No need for me to try to drive his truck wherever it was. It would be too easily spotted anyway. I walked Harvey briskly over to the passenger side and opened the door for him. He fell into the seat, and I buckled him in.

Chapter 19

On the one hand, I wanted to take him back to the office so I could sober him up enough for a good conversation, but on the other hand, I was in need of some documents for proof. I headed for his office at the dealership. Would he have been dense enough to put the documents I needed in such easy view? We would see.

Harvey was confused why we were at the dealership when we pulled into the parking lot.

"Whatr we doin' here? I thought you were goin' to get me a bottle."

"I thought you said you had one here ...in your desk drawer. Didn't you say that? Let's go look."

Harvey was cooperative. I like that in a drunk. We went into the building from the back. Inside the garage, there was a soft glow of lights coming from under one of the back rooms. I guessed that was where the gambling machines were. Luckily, no one was playing tonight. We made a turn into a hallway that led out to the waiting area for customers whose cars were being repaired in the garage. I didn't want to turn on any lights or otherwise attract attention, so we hit our share of walls. Of course, Harvey's lack of balance was not a bit of help. Somehow we managed to make it into his office, and he collapsed into his leather swivel chair behind his desk.

"Now, where is it?" I asked out loud as I began rummaging through the great big desk drawers. I wondered how long it would take Harvey to realize I was looking through papers and not looking for something as large as a bottle. About that time, he kicked the panel on the left side of the desk and a hidden wall popped open to reveal a bottle. Two, in fact, complete with glasses and mixers. Will wonders never cease? If there were one hidden panel, would there be two? So far, all I had come up with were regular business transactions in the papers I was searching.

"So Harvey, this is a clever set-up. Is this the only hidden compartment you have?"

"Yeah," he said as he picked up a glass with one hand and a bottle with the other. He poured himself a hefty-sized portion and took a huge swig. I'd better talk fast if I was going to get anything out of him before he passed out. I knew I'd never get him back to my office now, much less get him sober.

"Okay Harvey, tell me about Garth."

Harvey's eyes welled up with tears. Oh no, he was a crying drunk.

"He 'us my frien'," Garth sobbed.

"I know," I soothed. If he kept this up, I was never going to get anything out of him. He would start on a "Garth was a saint" eulogy and nothing would be accomplished. The spark of an idea ignited in my weary brain.

"Harvey, we need to get justice for Garth. Now help me figure out what he did to make those people so angry they would treat him this way."

His head wobbled up and he tried to look me in the eyes. He was probably seeing double at this point, but maybe the two of us could convince him.

"He … we …." Oh no, I could see it coming. Harvey's head collapsed on the desk. There was going to be a bruise, but he wouldn't feel it because of the intense headache he would have from all the liquor. By now, it was 1:00 A.M. I had hit the point when you are so exhausted your body can't turn off. I had less than seven hours to piece together what I thought had happened to Garth and Delago.

Eight o'clock was the magic hour. I was going to need corroboration from the coroner, but I was going to have to start here with the evidence that the two of them were connected. Harvey was going to be no help, but neither was he going to be a hindrance. The drool was starting to form at the edge of his mouth.

One of Edgar Allan Poe's stories, "The Purloined Letter" featured an antagonist who knew if you want to hide something, you could put it out in the open as if it were meant to be there. People broke into his house and searched all of the secret spaces they could find, never finding the letter. Why? It was right on the desk in plain view for all, especially himself, to see, and therefore, keep it safe.

I had nearly killed myself looking for another hidden compartment or some lock box or even a safe, all to no avail. I didn't think Harvey was that clever, so maybe he wasn't even trying to hide the evidence I needed. Maybe he hadn't bothered to conceal it.

That's when I hit the files in the cabinet. I started like I had at the office, with the most recent transactions. Even though I had a date for the sale of the property according to my notes and the subsequent stories, I knew there might be other transactions that would be beneficial to my evidence gathering.

I glanced at the clock, fully aware that each precious minute that slipped away without the right documents meant I was going to lose this chance to redeem myself to Billy, and better still, see to it that these criminals had a proper adversary. Duplicity was their cloak to hide under. This backdoor dealing was not a fair fight.

"Not in my town," was my rallying cry.

The first file contained all the paperwork for purchasing for the month. The subsequent ones looked just about the same in order by back date. It became monotonous to go through the same purchase orders: tires, mufflers, belts, radiators, batteries, fans, and oil filters. My overworked brain started making rhymes and sing songs with the items. By the tenth file, I was losing my mind in: "The Wheels of the Dealer Go Round and Round."

Suddenly, I realized I wasn't looking in the right place. These purchases were for the items he needed in the garage. He had told me part of the purchase price for the land included the sale of trucks. That was what I needed. Now I could dispense with these files easily and really get to work.

By 3:30 A.M. I was knee deep in files that were no help, and I could probably run Harvey's garage myself with all I had learned from the paperwork I had gone through. At least narrowing the focus had made the load more manageable. I was rapidly reaching the point where I thought maybe I had made a mistake about finding any documentation. It would have been foolish for Harvey to leave something that incriminating around. He had not moved at all since falling on his head. He was snoring, so I knew he was still alive.

I sure could have used a cup of coffee, but I thought it would be unconscionable to try to find evidence of criminal activity in a man's office and make coffee in his coffee maker at the same time.

Wait a minute! Caffeine didn't just come in coffee form, and we had passed by a customer lounge on the way in here. I'd bet three truck bills of sale that a Coke machine was in there and I could get a Mountain Dew or some other high-powered drink, like Red Bull.

I made my way down the hall where a faint light ebbed from the machine in the corner of the customer lounge. I was in luck, plenty of cold caffeine. I plunked the coins in the slot and punched the large button on a Dr. Pepper, picking up the can and popping the lid open when it slid down the chute. As I was turning around to head back to Harvey's office, I saw a flash of light from inside the garage and glancing off the wall down the hall.

Chapter 20

Was somebody here? Uh-oh, was it the city police looking for Harvey because his truck was still at The Blue Moon? Or, was it the security guard? Either way, I was going to be in big trouble if they found me here. I had to think quickly, and at nearly 4:00 A.M., low on caffeine, and nervous adrenaline, that was going to be a challenge.

The nearest door won my selection choice of the doors I could see. I raced over to it, tried the handle, and found it was locked. I tried the next one. Locked. My luck was running out. The glow of light I'd seen was now a beam, and I was relatively certain it was a flashlight. It was aiming down the hallway next to the customer lounge, bouncing as it came.

There, above me, shining as a light from heaven, was a sign that read "Ladies." I opened the door as quietly as I could and slipped inside. I went as stealthily as possible over to a stall and climbed on the commode. If, for any reason, the security guard decided he needed to take a peek in the Ladies Room, he would not see anyone inside. I could drink my drink while I waited.

And I waited … and waited … and waited.

Did I dare take a look outside? I had to. My time was running out. I slipped off my shoes, so I would be in my bare feet. I knew what they said about the floors being the nastiest part of the bathroom, but I would pull out the bleach later. I tiptoed to the door and pulled it open slowly until just a centimeter showed the hallway outside. It looked dark, but that could be deceptive because the guard might be in Harvey's office.

Gosh, I was glad I was a neat investigator. I had put all the files back after searching them and closed the drawers. Harvey's office would look as it had when we arrived.

One of my better qualities is patience. I was happy to give Mr. Security Guard all the time he needed, since it would not impress Billy if I was both arrested for trespassing *and* had nothing to give him. But there it was, the perpetual clock of life, with the time ticking away.

After an eternity of waiting had come and gone, the beam of light resurrected into the hall once more. The Security Guard moved slowly past the bathroom door. I had eased the door closed when I saw him coming, and was watching a sliver of light pass by under it. I thought his easy pace indicated that he had either seen Harvey in an accustomed state, or he hadn't seen him at all.

I engaged more patience as I watched the seconds tick away to be sure I didn't open the door and alert the guard I was here.

Opening Harvey's door once more, I saw his head still in the same position. He emitted a moan. I stepped inside, and tried to see the room from a fresh perspective. A little bit of caffeine began flowing in my bloodstream. If I had a truck receipt that was important, would I hide it or leave it out in the open? And if I hid it, where would I hide it? More caffeine was making its way into my brain. Harvey wouldn't have hidden it. He wouldn't have realized it was a damning piece of evidence, and he would have let his secretary file it just like it was any other receipt. Since he sold and purchased trucks on a regular basis, it wouldn't have looked the least bit suspicious to her. My mistake had been in not looking in the vehicle purchase files. Like the secretary, I had assumed those files were not important. It was 4:35 A.M. Better get started.

When I came up for air an hour later, I knew that the most commonly sold car at Harvey Layfield's dealership was a midsize sedan. Trucks were second on the list because this was a town where all the men had a truck whether they needed it or not. The semis were buried in the same month as the purchase on the property, September of last year. If memory served me right, that was the same month I had seen Garth in the big city near Morton with his friend. After that, a regular stream of shady characters had been in Garth's company. If I had paid closer attention, I could have alerted Billy, and may have averted this trouble.

The semis were not the only unusual thing Harvey had purchased. I found all kinds of receipts in the stack of files that, taken one at a time, would have signaled nothing, but collectively were putting together a picture of a lot of spending. I would never have kept such receipts in my office, but if Harvey were laundering money, this would be the place to do it.

After all, he was well known in Morton, so transactions of large amounts of money at the local bank would have put up a red flag, so transacting everything with cash would have been smart. He was doing a lot of traveling back and forth to Vegas. The company credit card must have been sizzling with all the transactions on it. I doubted Harvey was making all that money from winning at the black jack table. He didn't strike me as the lucky type.

So, where was all the money coming from? And it was cash. Let's see. Lots of money, cash, all unaccounted for, a trucking company trying hard to blend in and look legitimate. Transporting antiques? My style, and maybe Garth's, but certainly not Harvey's. Besides, that kind of illegal activity was too cumbersome.

No, people buy semis for two reasons. One was the legitimate transportation of legitimate goods. The other was illegal activity. The purchase of these semis was for either illegal immigration or drugs. That had to be it. Now that I had the connection, I was going to need to substantiate my theory with more facts, and that would happen at the opening of the business day, at 8:00 A.M. I went over to Harvey because it is illegal to take someone else's property without their permission. I pulled my tape recorder out of my purse and switched it on.

"Harvey, is it okay with you if I make a copy of this bill of sale and these receipts?" I asked.

Harvey didn't answer. I shook his arm.

"Harvey!"

"Whhhaaa," he mumbled.

"I said, is it okay if I make a copy of this bill of sale and these receipts?"

"Yeh. Mmm." Or something like that. Remind me not to drink. People can coerce you into things if you do. I switched off the recorder and availed myself of the copier behind his desk, replacing the bill of sale in the file, along with the other papers I had copied. I tucked my copies into my purse and heaved a weary sigh. It was 5:42 and counting. I headed for the door.

When I was a kid, I had read all about the American Indians who were originally located in my home state. One of the things that impressed me about them was their skilled stealth. I used to practice moving through the house without my mom knowing. She had very sharp eyes and ears, so getting by her was a challenge. I was glad I had played that childhood game because it was paying off now.

The world begins to stir at 6:00 A.M., and I was taking an awful chance of being seen leaving in the early dawn light. I slipped out of the building's garage, and quickened my pace to my car. It was about then I realized that my movements had probably been caught on security cameras, anyway. No more wasting time trying not to be seen or heard, I was bold as brass as I swiftly exited the parking lot.

I did a drive-by photo op at Harvey Layfield's house. I was sure this was going to figure into the evidence pile, and since I was already out and about, it would save time later. That was the most important thing, to manage the precious time I had left.

Chapter 21

When I inserted my key into the back door at *The World* office, the handle was pulled from my grip by a hand from within. I stared into the lovely green eyes of my son. He was standing there with one hand on the door handle and the other on his hip. At that moment, he looked just like my dad. I felt a catch in my throat.

"Alright missy, and just where have you been all night? And don't try telling me you were spending the night at your friend's house because we called all of your friends, and you weren't there."

"Hi honey," I said as I brushed past him and headed for my desk. "Can't talk right now. Lots to do."

"Mom, do you realize the girls are worried sick? They called me to come home from school because they couldn't find you."

"I'm sorry, honey, but I have to get this information in order. Please tell them I will explain everything this afternoon, but right now, time is running out."

While I talked I put my purse down on my desk, opened up my files and started digging through the notes from last September. My son shook his head in disbelief.

"Mom, did you hear me? The girls are worried sick. You didn't come home last night. Your cell phone was off and you didn't check your messages and call us back. The girls knew you were upset. You said something about going to the office, and took off."

"I know honey. I'm sorry. Please, just let me get this done." I planted a kiss on his cheek. "Please."

He looked at me and shrugged. "Okay. What can I do?"

"First, go take care of the girls. Assure them I am all right, and I'm sorry for upsetting them. I promise I'll be home when they get back from school, and I'll explain everything then. Tell them I know about the van."

My terse explanation and directions must have sufficed because he hurried out the back door. I started pulling pertinent files out and loading them on my desk. To get a sense of the time frame, I pulled out a legal pad and started assigning dates to the events that marked the significant pieces to the puzzle and established a timeline. By doing so, I would be sure to collect all of the offending insects in the net.

First, was the sale of the land and the trucks, then the construction of the buildings that would develop the industrial park. Next, was the beginning of the trucking company and with the trucks purchased from Harvey. These were being used to transport goods.

Garth had brought in outside help for this project back in September. He had made frequent trips to the city on business for Morton. I had this in my notes from the city council meetings. Just like Edgar Allan Poe's nefarious criminal, he had hidden the evidence of his actions in the open. It looked like legitimate business was being conducted. The witching hour had arrived.

I picked up my cell phone and consulted my journalist's directory. Maniacs, menaces, munchies, here it was: morgue. As soon as the second hand hit the twelve on the clock, and it had turned 8:00 A.M., the time for all normal people to be at work, I punched in the numbers to speak to our coroner.

The coroner's table is the Judgment Day of this world. There is nothing hidden on it. Did you have a surgery no one knew about? An aborted pregnancy? A drug or alcohol problem? Did you eat something you weren't supposed to for dinner? Well, there it is for all to see. There are no more secrets, no more lies, no more collusion. The coroner has all knowledge, and he's going to share it.

"Mike?" I asked tremulously, less for speaking to our coroner than anxious for the answer I needed.

"Yeah?"

"This is Mibbie Wright, with *The World*."

"Oh, Hi. What can I do for you?"

"Do you have Garth's body yet?"

"Uh ….."

He paused. Not good. When someone pauses in answer to a question, they are thinking of an answer or they don't want to answer the question. Since I had asked Mike a "yes" or "no" kind of question, I knew his hesitation was the latter. If I met one more person I was going to have to *make* talk, in addition to the people already on my list, I was going to get out my bludgeoning stick.

"Mibbie, I'm not sure I …."

"Never mind, Mike, I get it. How about Delago Fuentez?"

"Well, gee Mibbie, you found him."

"Yeah, but there was something I forgot to take a picture of."

"What?"

"His body."

"His body?"

"Yeah, did you take a picture?"

"Well, yeah, lots of them, what was left of it."

"Can you get them out for me?"

"Sure, hold on a minute?"

The song "Rescue Me" was playing while I waited. Déjà vu, as I hummed to this tune. I wondered if the "On Hold" guys had delivered the same recording track to all the people of this town.

"Okay, I got them. What are you looking for?" Mike said when he got back on the line.

"Not sure yet, but could you look at them and tell me about anything strange you see, maybe on the web of his hand, in between the thumb and the forefinger?"

"Alright. Looking. Nope, nothing there."

"The rest of him?"

"Well, he was pretty mauled. Hmmm. There is something here on his shoulder. A tattoo. Kind of strange looking. Yeah, there seem to be two numbers there. And there are wings over here."

"Can you tell what they are, the numbers, I mean?"

"Let's see, hard to make out, but I think it's a one and a three."

"What about the wings?"

"There are, well, I think these are wings, and a name is beside them."

"Are the wings above the name?"

"Yeah."

"Great. And Mike? Would you at least answer a 'yes' or 'no' question for me? For old times sake?"

"Gee, Mibbie...I..."

"Just 'yes' or 'no'. Was there anything marked on Garth? Carved into him, or burned into him. Something like that?"

His hesitation was so long, I thought we had been disconnected. I was afraid to say anything for fear he was making up his mind and my words would put him off. I was afraid to even exhale.

Then it came. A whisper.

"Yes, a number 13."

Chapter 22

I had to breathe deeply for ten minutes and drink two glasses of water for the next phone call. I don't do confrontations very well. This next bit of business was going to be tricky. I'd seen Sam Waterston, on *Law and Order,* and Perry Mason, in his courtroom, do it a thousand times. My hero Sam Spade wouldn't even have to do it. He'd just slap the guy around to get what he wanted.

I was going to have to make someone tell on himself. I had been pretty good at it as an educator and a parent; let's see how I did as a journalist. As a teacher, I'd say something like this: "We'll just see what your mom thinks about that." Then the child would go home and ask, "What did Ms. Wright say when she called?" The parent would say, "Why would Ms. Wright have to call?"

I had already been over to the tax assessor's office at the courthouse and looked up the information I needed about the property at the industrial park. I must have set a record with how fast I was going. Still, I was on schedule, and not early as I had hoped, but, at least, not late. We were going to print today and I had to check out all my facts before I even wrote my story. I rehearsed my mantra: "Just do the next thing."

At 8:20, I called Senator Hughes's office.

Chapter 23

"Hi, this is Mibbie Wright from *The World*, is the Senator in?"

"Well, yes, Ms. Wright, and considering the news about Mr. Miller that shows his dedication. The Senator is absolutely grief stricken," his ever-loyal and probably paid-a-pretty-penny-for-it secretary sang out melodiously.

Great! I'd be in like Flynn. Wondered who Flynn was, but really, just wanted in.

I purred.

"Of course he is. Such a shock. They were great friends, and I know he must be broken to pieces, but as you know, we will be doing the obituary and it just wouldn't be proper to write one without some comforting words for our reading public from the man they all admire."

I wondered if that was enough smoke and mirrors to do it or if I would have to say more. Frankly, that first bit had turned my stomach. If any more was required, I was going to need to borrow Steve's Pepto.

"Of course," the secretary soothed. "Let me see if he can see you."

She was back on the line in a minute. Not a surprise since I was sure that a request to be the center of attention was probably high on Senator Hughes's list of acceptable things to ask him to do.

"He'll see you at 9:00 A.M. sharp. He has a very busy schedule."

"Of course, he does. I'll be there right on time."

The truth was, I needed more time. If I was going to spring my trap, woman's intuition wasn't going to get it. I needed easels and powerpoint presentations, maps and one of those light-up pointy things. Time to scramble, which I did pretty well, having had a lot of practice with my errant parenting ways, leading to last minute scrambles for science project materials or classroom presentation copies.

At 8:59 sharp, I was seated in the law office of Hughes, Suffolk and Hughes. Like most politicians, Senator Hughes had a daytime job where he pretended to make all the money the poor taxpayers were forking out for his over-inflated salary including the senatorial bonuses and raises he and the rest of his brethren had voted themselves in the last two budget cuts. Nobody on the payroll was taking those cuts seriously. It only affected the state services offered to the taxpayers who, to put it in Steve's words, "Let them do it, so they must think it is okay."

The walls and furniture of Senator Hughes's waiting room were appropriately bland. One thing was for certain, he wasn't decorating using that huge senatorial paycheck. This must have been reassuring to the constituents who visited him. His secretary was busy typing on her keyboard and answering numerous phone calls. She said the same thing to every person, so much so that I started to offer to recite it for her.

Nine o'clock came and went. I sure could have used that

extra time to prepare for my presentation.

Finally, that big bear of a man with a boisterous voice and matching personality came looming in the doorframe.

"Sorry to keep you waitin' Mizz Wright, but I'm sure you know there are so many details to see about."

"Of course, Senator. This is just one more. A simple obituary just won't do. We'll need your personal influence to tell the story right."

With that saccharine spoonful of honey, he issued me into the sanctuary of his office.

"Have a seat there, Mizz. Wright. May I offer you somethin'? Cold drink? Coffee? Tea?"

"No sir. I don't want to take up too much of your valuable time. Let's get right down to business, so I don't detain you from your important work."

"I like a girl who knows her mind."

What a consummate politician. Flattering me without any need to!

"So Senator, how long have you and Mr. Miller known one another?"

"Garth, …may I call him that? We were very old and dear friends. I hope the familiarity doesn't offend you. I want to be respectful of his position in this community."

"Oh no, please, do go on."

The Senator smiled one of his most magnanimous smiles, the kind I was sure he reserved for the people who were about to do him a big favor. He settled back in his leather-bound chair with his hands clasped before him, fingers interlaced, looking up at the ceiling in a far-off thoughtful gaze.

"Garth and I have known one another for years now. I'd say we go back at least fifteen years from when I knew his daddy. It was clear from our first meeting that Garth was a go-getter, progressive, I think you young people call him."

Oh, good. Now he was patronizing me about my age. He continued.

"Let's see, I think our first project together was the expansion of the marketing ventures around here. Together we got the state to pitch in some funding for some development of the local roadways. They were in such poor shape, horse and buggy must have used them."

He chuckled at his own joke. What an actor. Canned laughter couldn't have done it better.

"We found some land and bought it up, and the two of us developed an industrial park, the first one in the county, all for the betterment of this city. Progress, and all that. Yes, sir, I think Garth did so much for this little town and the county it resides in. I was proud to know him and call him my friend."

"And that land for the industrial park would have belonged to Harvey Layfield?"

"Well, I don't know... I ...uh ...guess." Senator Hughes was brought up short from his reminiscing. He hadn't expected me to say anything, just sit there and listen to his everlasting voice sing the praises of Garth Miller. He eyed me carefully. When I want to, I can put on an angelic smile. I did that now.

"Please go on," I said reassuringly.

At least my interruption had put a stop to him waxing rhapsodic.

"As I was saying. We made this county a better place by improving our little city. We brought jobs here, promoted the economy, fed the public service coffers. Garth Miller was a visionary who could see the way to grow a place."

Senator Hughes resumed, but the poetry in his recital ceased to glow. This must have been what happened when one of his constituents proposed the very unhappy prospect of disagreeing with him.

"And you paid Harvey Layfield 2.5 million for that land. Is that right?"

"What?"

"I said."

"I heard what you said. I thought you were here to talk about Garth Miller. What does that business deal have to do with Garth's death?"

"Were you aware that Harvey was paid that much?"

"Of course I was."

But I could tell by the way he said it, he was calculating. No, he wasn't.

"Now, did you put up the bonds for what the state funds didn't cover to repair those roads?" I could see he was starting to get angry, either by being put on the spot, or because he was starting to suspect I knew something he didn't want me to know.

"That is none of your business, young lady. I thought you were here for a story on Garth. If you just want to nose around, you can do that elsewhere."

"In fact, Senator, that is just what I have been doing, nosing around."

I slid a copy of the plat book from the County Assessor's Office in front of him. I followed it up with a Tax Assessor's card showing the value of the property.

"Public Access and all that. And unless I have completely misjudged your latest business venture, I would say you want to hear this story of mine so you don't end up like Garth. Or, do you like being executed?"

He was stunned, I could tell, but I also knew he was scared. It was so pleasant to have someone else in the hot seat for a change. This was my moment of glory. I could see Sam Spade leaning up against the wall over in the corner, striking a match on his shoe and lighting his hand-rolled cigarette. He smiled that enigmatic smile of his and told me with his eyes to go on; I had him!

"Well Senator, the reason I needed to know how long you and Garth have known each other is to know how long your jail term is going to be. It seems your friend Garth was throwing around a lot of money, and I'm not sure how much of it was yours. Having given him money that was used for illegal purposes makes you an accessory to his crimes. Legitimately, you make a hefty sum, but you and Garth both have documented only this much."

I slid a copy of the financial disclosure forms they filed when they ran for office. I had uncovered them from my files, having acquired them as part of my "all the facts" mentality for the stories I wrote on them during the campaign for election. In this case, it had paid off, being a piece of evidence I had not had to track down for this confrontation. I continued.

"The 2.5 million was just for starters; you probably didn't know how much Garth was passing around. You thought Layfield was only paid one million. It shocks you that he got that much, I know, but more? You hadn't counted on that. What you didn't know was that he got that much because land was not all Garth got in that deal. You know the land isn't worth that much anyway so why would Garth have given him all that money?"

I slid a bill of sale across to him. It showed the purchase of twelve semi's with trailers that I had found in Harvey's office early this morning. I followed it up with some more copies of the receipts I had uncovered to assist him in understanding this next part.

"Mr. Layfield is a drinking man, not sure if you knew that, but since Garth's murder, he seems to have taken to indulging himself even more. Drinking men tend to talk. He is scared, Senator. It seems his and Garth's new business enemies don't play nice, and he wasn't aware of that.

"When he started seeing the money roll in, Mr. Layfield thought the two of them could just muscle out the competition like he'd done in every shady business deal he's ever been involved in. But I can tell you Senator, Mr. Layfield would rather go to jail for fraud and drug trafficking than to end up in the back of his Chevy F-10 with his tongue cut out and his body carved up. You did know that was how they found Garth, right?"

Senator Hughes was the picture of attentiveness. He had

146

sat forward to look at the documents I kept sliding toward him. I could tell when he heard new information because his head jerked up to look into my face. This last statement obviously shocked him. No one knew the details of the body, yet. We hadn't run the story, and while some things go on the gossip telegraph before we get a chance to print it, nobody but me had made the connection.

When I saw Jorge, I knew MS 13 had made its way into our town. When I asked Mike about Garth's body, the telltale execution style along with the gang's markings let me know Garth had crossed them. The Senator was used to playing hardball with politicians who could be intimidated by power or bribed with favors, not gangs who were not intimidated by a loss of life and bribed by nothing.

"One of the businesses you and Garth set up is a trucking company, isn't it Senator? Or didn't you know that? It is located at the far end of the city industrial park, away from prying eyes. I passed it on my way here. It looks perfectly benign. I'll bet you didn't even know it was there and that you were a part owner in it.

"It's just another non-descript little trucking company, but it has your name on it: Hughes Enterprises. It has a nice ring to it. Too bad, you can't advertise because the people who are using your trucking company don't like publicity. Well, you wouldn't either if you were involved in illegal activity, which sadly, by virtue of your business dealings, you are."

I slid copies of pictures I had taken at dawn's early light of the building with the name emblazoned on the side. I watched as the color fled out of the good Senator's face. They had not only been using his money, they had been using his name.

"So, Mr. Layfield and Garth set up this trucking company with lots of pretty trucks, but they aren't brand new because that would draw attention to them. Your business partners needed to be discreet. Mr. Layfield's big mistake was throwing around his money. People can't help but notice something like that. So, he sells you and Garth the land, then he builds himself a mansion, puts in a pool, buys a brand new truck, takes vacations out to Las Vegas, and we all know they encourage you to come, not so you can win, but so you can lose.

"People are greedy, Senator Hughes. I don't know if you know that. When someone has a lead on how to get rich quick, other people want a piece of the action. People start to take an interest in where all this money comes from. The real estate agent would like her share of the cut of that property you bought."

I slid pictures of the Layfield compound showing Harvey's home and surrounding investments across his desk beside the receipts I had already put there. I was glad for the technology of a cell phone that takes pictures and then being able to print them out. Short of a powerpoint, I thought this visual aid part of the confrontation was a nice touch. "Are you getting all this Senator? If not, don't worry. I have more files over at the office. It took me all night to go through all my old stories and notes to see how all this adds up."

"I have never seen a story on any of this," the Senator thundered. I had to hand it to him. Even under pressure, he still tried to appear commanding.

"Now Senator. You are a politician. When you are making all those state deals, do you put all your cards on the table? No, of course you don't. You play your aces close to your chest. This is all background work for a larger story."

I slid a clipping of the Senator and Garth at Garth's Mayoral Inauguration across the desk and smiled.

"You two go way back don't you? There's a new member of the community. He's a DEA agent, who just happens to be working on the drug trafficking in our area. Seems we have a little drug smuggling going on around here. And that's where all the pieces fit together. Your trucking agency is being used to transport drugs in between the two bustling metropolises on either side. How do you like that? And you were going to give Garth your job. Some payback, huh?"

I worded the allusion to the DEA agent in such a way as to make Senator Hughes believe we were already collaborating. It was a bluff. Since I always get caught in my lies, I figured this near-lie, buried in all the legitimate stuff, would slip by. The DEA would be involved somewhere along the line. I already knew from Billy that they had an undercover operation going on, and that the agent working on the case had made the connection between drug activity and gang activity after my Corn Dog debacle.

The Senator was torn between rage and shock. Being accustomed to the way things worked at the capitol, he thought he had manipulated the situation, but Garth had manipulated him. I wasn't sure if he was more angry about the money he could have had, but lost, or more angry that his political reputation had been sullied by a couple of would-be drug lords. He sputtered a bit.

"Don't worry, Senator," I said. "You don't need to give a public statement at this time; I've got it all on tape!"

With that, I held up my tape recorder.

"I haven't admitted to anything."

"No, but you haven't denied it either. And as you know, I always get my facts right, so the story I will write will include any quotes you care to make, otherwise, I'll just say you were unavailable for comment and use this conversation as verification for your part in all this. Of course, you will be unavailable for comment, after they arrest you, that is."

I paused waiting for a response. "Nothing? Okay, I'll be seeing you."

It was so much fun sashaying out of his office. I even paused at the door to toss my hair at him. Gosh, I love my job sometimes.

Chapter 24

My cell phone rang almost as soon as I got out of the door. Steve had as good a nose for news as he had for timing.

"How'd it go? Did he flinch? What did he say? Did you get it all on tape? Where are you now?"

"Fine. Yes. Nothing. Yes, and on my way back."

Steve had been able to find out from the city policeman who had reported finding Garth's body that an anonymous phone call had been made to the dispatcher late yesterday. In this day of caller ID and other recognition devices, I was puzzled by the term "anonymous." Really? I didn't buy that.

The caller had simply said, "You will find the mayor's body in his car at mile marker 231," then hung up.

Steve managed to find out the time of the call and more information than the city police wanted to give up through the masterful way he has of knowing something really questionable about everyone in town. This included the officer who took the call. From him, Steve was able to find out that Chief Putnam had been notified, but that the chief had dismissed the call as a prank. When they found the car and Garth's body inside, the chief had miraculously appeared, his earlier dismissal of the call as a hoax, apparently forgotten. The duty officer said he looked "shaken."

Even though Steve had contacted the chief, he hadn't

returned his phone calls. I would have bet a nasty lunch at The Inn and five hundred dollars, that Chief Putnam was "out of town." I would have won, too, because I only bet on a sure thing.

Steve was ready to pounce on me when I got back to the office; I barely had time to hang up my cell phone before I stepped inside the door.

"Give over"

"I'll do better than that," I said. "Listen to this."

I put my tape recorder on my desk and pressed "Play," glad I use an old fashioned device, so my cell phone is free.

Steve smiled as he listened to the conversation. He nodded at me when he heard me make my assertions. He laughed out loud when the Senator said he hadn't admitted anything.

"The rest is for lawyers and detectives, Mibbie. We've got our story."

"Not yet, Steve," I said. "I want to get a look at those trucks."

"Mildred Claire Wright! Haven't you caused enough trouble with that sheriff of yours? You will get yourself killed, and he won't be sorry. Besides, we've got to get these stories written."

"Okay, look. You and I both know, even though we don't have the proof right now, that the police chief and Garth were in this together. If the trucks were coming through here, they would have been immune to any scrutiny by the local law enforcement because of Chief Putnam's relationship with Garth, but what about Billy's boys?

"Would they have seen anything? If they were part of the cover-up, I want to know. If they were taking bribes to look the other way, how much trouble am I going to get into with Billy, if I find out for him instead of Billy having to find out for himself? Besides, we need to know with certainty that the trucking angle is right. We don't have anybody *on record* saying there is a connection. We just have pieces of a puzzle. I want to see the whole picture, and I want to see it finished."

"Okay, but I'm going with you."

Chapter 25

The industrial park in our small town was really just a collection of big buildings with various names on them on a huge stretch of pavement. It wasn't hard to find the Hughes Building, again. I hadn't exactly lied when I told Senator Hughes that I had driven by there on my way to see him; I had driven by there on my way from Harvey's house to my office. All I had really done was to read my old notes and know that it had been erected, and to get out the photos from the file I had done on my story of the industrial park before and after it was christened.

Fortunately, the Senator was too busy trying to get out from under my attack to take note of any hesitation on my part or to see any signs that my statements lacked voracity. What I *had* done was go by Harvey's house, knowing I would need pictures of his pretty new toys for my visual evidence collection. However, despite my not having personally seen the trucking company, my description of the location of it had been accurate. As for the name, I had found it on the truck invoices I had seen in Harvey's office. I don't like not being entirely honest, especially with my proclivity for being caught every time I do something wrong, or even think about doing something wrong.

The Hughes Enterprises building was at the back of the park. A truck was nestled in the delivery apron. Nobody was around. My victory with Senator Hughes had given me superhuman confidence, and I parked my car in a logical place alongside other cars near the building. Nothing conspicuous about me, no sir. Steve and I got out and circled around to the back of the car. If we had had a plan this would have been the time to give each other the codes for action. As it was, we just looked at each other, first, then around the empty, but for parked cars, parking lot.

I scanned for cameras. Almost every business these days does security surveillance as a matter of practice. There they were, top of the pole, probably filming both Steve and myself as we tried to play the role of common citizen. Something bold came over me and I walked over to the truck sitting at the loading dock. The dock door was closed; the truck cab was empty, and as I walked around it, I wondered what in the world I was doing? It was silly to think the culprits would have a truck standing wide open with drugs just sitting there for me to find.

I walked up the stairs to the loading dock and knocked on the door of the office. Of course, no one came to the door. What did I expect from a clandestine drug operation? Satisfied that Steve and I had accomplished absolutely nothing, I retraced my steps to my waiting boss.

"Nothing, huh?" he said.

"No, I didn't expect anything exactly, but I'd like to see the trucks in action. Want me to take you back to the office?"

"No. This is a lot of fun. We can let The Sports Guy handle things for a while."

"Do you really think this is a lot of fun or are you teasing me that we came up with nothing?"

"No, really Mibs, this is fun, stalking non-moving trucks and knocking on doors that don't open and learning absolutely nothing of value about our lead."

I punched him in the arm.

"Get in, wise guy."

We pulled out of the parking lot. I wasn't sure which way to turn, but figured that if the trucks were going to be traveling, they would probably be going to and from the interstate. I had to hand it to Garth. His plan was ingenious. He had purchased this land in the midst of a financial crunch and brought business to our town. He had been hailed as a hero by the community, while lining his own pockets.

I hadn't actually talked to the DEA agent who had gotten involved when I had my run-in at The Corn Dog. Except that I was allowed to know there was drug trafficking going on in this area, and that there was an on-going investigation, and that there was a DEA agent in our area. Other than that, my knowledge was still cave dark.

So, what I told Senator Hughes was just confirmation of those facts. Aligning it to Garth's trucking venture had been a figment of my vivid imagination, but luckily, as it turned out, a correct one. Given the Senator's reaction and Mr. Layfield's sudden reliance on liquid courage, I had hit the target right on the mark. Of course, the price of that knowledge had been the scolding I got from Billy after I had careened into the Corn Dog with hopes flying high that I could deliver something to make up for my previous mistakes.

We weren't actually on speaking terms, the DEA agent working on the case and I, even if I had misled Senator Hughes into thinking that.

I headed right, to the interstate, scanning the side streets to see where I might pull over for a stake out. The truck we had seen parked in the loading dock at the building was one of three things: a truck emptying its load; a truck picking up its load; or, a truck that was a decoy, and I had fallen for it. Of course, it might have been a truck that was not in working order, but I felt that drug lords probably kept their trucks in peak condition. It simply didn't make sense to make a drug run with a truck that broke down on the interstate.

A huge, drooping wisteria vine in full bloom that hung from an old oak was the perfect hiding spot. I pulled over and turned around in someone's driveway to park under it. Wisterias are nature's strangulation artists. They look so lovely and are so fragrant that no one wants to get rid of them. But, the next thing you know, your trees are dying a slow and agonizing death. The delicate, little purple flowers look like pea pods. I didn't have to roll down the window to drink in their perfume, because my car window was still broken, one of the many things I had neglected to take care of in pursuit of a good lead.

Steve was not very impressed with nature. He tried to sit still. He fidgeted with the radio, my CD collection, and my notebook, but I drew the line at him rummaging through my purse.

"Stop that," I said, sounding like a scolding mother.

"Do you have anything to eat?" And Steve sounded like

a spoiled child.

"No, of course not. Remember, I'm the mom who can be brought up on starvation charges for my children."

"Yeah, but women always have something to eat in their purses."

"Well, I don't. Now sit still, or I'm not going to let you play stake-out with me."

"Mibbie, did you think about what we'll do if we see one of those trucks?"

"Follow it."

"Why?"

"To see where it goes and what happens when it stops."

"Billy's detectives get paid to do this. Why don't you let them?"

"Nobody made you come along."

"I thought you were on to something."

"I know, you only want me when I have an exciting lead."

"Listen, I've got to get back to the paper. This has been fun, but we've got to go to print. I still haven't finished my story, and you have to write yours. I'll even share the front page with you. What do you say? Ready to pack in the deputy act?"

Steve was right. I had wanted a front-page story, and I had gotten it. Billy had already had enough of me trying to do his job. I wasn't paid to do it, trained to do it, and so far I hadn't done anything right. I started the car, intent on doing the right thing, but just then, a "Hughes Trucking" semi rolled past us.

I looked at Steve and smiled. We followed the truck.

Chapter 26

Going back into the parking lot behind the semi was too obvious, so I gave him a long lead. Steve had pulled out my camera and was attaching the wide-angle lens. I was glad I had him along because my heart was racing. I shuddered to think what would have happened to that expensive piece of equipment in my trembling hands. We slowed to a near crawl. Good fortune smiled; another car was approaching from the opposite direction. When it turned into the parking lot of the industrial park, giving me the opportunity to do the same, but without the truck driver seeing only me, it seemed too good to be true. When it drove down to the end of the blacktop where the Hughes Trucking Company was and parked across from the truck, I knew *it was too good to be true.*

The semi went to the end of the parking lot and backed into the loading dock next to the truck already stationed there. The car that had preceded us, parked on the opposite side of the truck.

"Pull over," Steve said.

"What?"

Before I could ask him again, he had jumped out, taken several shots with the camera over the roof of my car as I came to a screeching halt, and approached the semi. What nerves of steel this boss of mine had!

"Hey, mind if I ask you a couple of questions?" he asked the driver who was swinging down from the cab.

"Don't have time for no questions," the trucker replied.

"No time? I'll walk with you."

The driver reached behind him and grabbed his jacket out of the truck.

"I don't got nothin' to say to you."

"You will when the police get here."

The driver stopped in his tracks. "Why would the cops be comin'?"

"Do you know what is in your truck?"

"I'm paid to drive it, not check its contents," the driver said as he started towards the car we had followed into the parking lot.

"Don't you know you are responsible for its contents?"

"Yeah, gettin' it from one place to another. Which I did." He stopped at the car and put his hand on the door handle, ready to end his conversation with Steve.

"So, you don't sign a contract stating what is in the truck? Do you know what a bill of lading is?"

"Well, I … Hey, who are you?"

"I'm the editor of the local newspaper. You will find yourself in a lot of trouble if you aren't careful."

I was too busy watching this interchange to see someone walk behind my car. And I was too engrossed in this compelling conversation to see that same someone sidle up to my window.

"Do you think it is possible to keep your nose out of my

business?" asked a voice at my elbow. From the credentials he had planted in front of my face, I could see it was my friendly local DEA agent, the one I had never met. That is … until now.

I nearly jumped out of my skin.

"I'm not doing anything," I said, sounding as unconvincing as a teenager with a beer in his hand at a traffic stop.

"No, you aren't doing anything *this* time. You got your buddy involved, and now *he* is making a mess of my investigation."

"No, we were just trying…"

"What's his name?"

"Who?"

"Your buddy."

"Steve."

"Wait a minute, how did you know we'd be here?"

But he didn't answer, just called to Steve who was getting himself into a lather with the truck driver. Steve was trying to convince the driver to talk to him, and the truck driver was resisting. When the DEA agent called his name, Steve wheeled around, shocked at hearing another male voice when he was pretty sure the only other two people in the parking lot were female: me in my car, and Mr. Truck Driver's companion in hers.

The DEA agent walked over to Steve and put his arm around his shoulder, walking him back to my car. He paused long enough to call back over his own shoulder to the truck driver.

"Go on home. This will all be straightened out in the morning."

The truck driver was grateful enough, and got in the passenger side of the car that had come for him. By the time they were pulling out of the parking lot, Steve and the DEA agent had reached my car. The agent walked Steve around to the passenger side of the car and opened the door continuing the conversation he had begun with him when he retrieved him from his terrier attack on the unhelpful truck driver. Steve obediently got in.

"So, you see, we are in the midst of an investigation that could be harmed if you aren't discreet. I can assure you, we will find out all the information you need for a good story. I understand your local sheriff has a good working relationship with your paper, and I don't have a problem helping you out when it doesn't compromise what we are working on, but right now, you two are running right up against our case. Do you think you could find something else to keep you occupied for a little while?"

What he said was the sort of thing that sounded condescending to grown-ups. I thought Steve would probably get angry, but he seemed all right with it.

"Sorry," Steve said.

I was too amazed to speak. The DEA agent leaned down and looked across the passenger side to me.

"Are you always this much trouble?"

"Oh, please let me answer this, Mibbie," Steve interjected. "Yes, she is."

"Will you two stop talking to me as if I were a child?" I

163

replied indignantly. " And by the way, Steve, as I recall, you were the one who wanted to come along, the one who jumped out and confronted the truck driver, and the one who had to be fetched back to the car. I am still here, thank you very much!"

"Only because you were too scared to take him on," Steve shot back.

"Alright, you two, stop bickering like children. Why don't you head on back to the newspaper and write up all this wonderful newsworthy stuff you've been gathering. Leave the drug investigation to me. Here's my card. When you feel the desire to investigate drug activity around here, resist it, and just call me, your hardworking drug investigator. Got it?" He handed his card to Steve.

"Does Bil..., I mean Sheriff Bartlett, have to know?" I asked more plaintively than I meant to sound.

That smug, self-appointed babysitter of a DEA agent laughed.

"No, young lady, Sheriff Bartlett doesn't have to know. Would you be grounded if he did?"

I hissed back in my most venomous fashion, "Oh my goodness. I had no idea stand-up comedy was part of your gig. But really, you shouldn't give up your day job, yet."

I was incensed. Grounded, indeed! Young Lady, I'll tell you! At least my time with Steve had paid off enough to come up with one smart aleck response. Hopefully, the DEA agent would let it drop after my single sentence tongue blistering. I didn't think there was another verbal jab left in me.

"Well, with you messing up my cases, I have to have some way of earning my keep. But, I'll tell you what. If you go about your business as a reporter, I'll try to go about mine cleaning up the drugs in this town. Deal?"

I decided to show my displeasure at his overbearing comments by not answering. Steve, who was not the picture of loyalty, said, "Just let us know when we can have the story. And by the way, I've already got the pictures to go with it."

This was his way of ensuring an exclusive. If the DEA didn't share information, Steve would print a story anyway, using his pictures and the information he did have. If the DEA agent shared the information with our rival paper, Steve had pictures and a story they didn't have. I started the car and pulled away. Steve chattered happily all the way back to the office, but I couldn't get past the sick feeling in my stomach that Billy was going to find out I had once again been meddling.

Chapter 27

I made a beeline for the Sheriff's Department when we got back. Steve had yelled out the door after me to hurry back so I could get the Senator Hughes story ready for the front page. I was relieved to see that Gayle was manning the front desk; she hadn't taken lunch yet.

"Mibbie," she said, by way of greeting.

"Gayle, is Billy in?"

"Mibbie, honey, do you think this is a good time?"

"Gayle, I believe I have been redeemed. I have a story Billy will be reading on the front page, but I am sure he would like to hear about it from me first. Besides, we are in the midst of an investigation, and he needs me."

"Did you say 'We'?"

"Yes."

"Now Mibbie, you know I would never hurt your feelings intentionally, but Billy has made it quite clear that you are not a detective and should you come for a job interview as one, I am to tell you the position has been filled!"

"Oh, Gayle. Don't you see? I'm not trying to do detective work. I'm trying to give him the information I have so *he* can. Look, it's all right here in my notes."

I held up the huge collection of dated material, notebooks, newspaper clippings and photocopies that in someone else's hand might have looked like a garbage heap or a recycling bag at best.

"Let me see if he'll talk to you."

"No! I have a better idea. Get me the one honest investigator Billy has."

"There isn't one."

"Okay, get Billy, but Gayle? Please tell him I just want to give him information, not get any."

In a minute, or so, Gayle stepped back into the hall from Billy's office and curled her finger twice with the universal sign of summoning someone. I followed her back to Billy's office. He was sitting at his desk, his feet propped up on the windowsill behind him, talking on the phone. When he swiveled around, he looked weary, and I was sorry that some of the worry lines on his face had been etched there by my fine hand. The remnants of breakfast were still sitting on his desk, mostly untouched, but not a healthy breakfast anyway.

Gayle pointed to the chair in front of him, and I sat down, some of my unkempt paper fluttering to the floor. Gayle knelt down to help me gather it back up in a mass on my lap.

"You aren't going to try to show him all this, are you?" she whispered, so as not to disturb Billy's phone conversation.

"No, just the stuff he needs, and not even that, if he is willing to take my word for what I have to tell him," I whispered back.

"It isn't that he doesn't trust you, Mibbie," Gayle said soulfully.

"I know," I said. "I know what I need to do to make things right. I'll do my job as a reporter and leave the law enforcement to him, I promise. I'm really sorry for all the trouble I've caused. I just want to help, now, really"

Gayle smiled back reassuringly, patted me on the arm, and left the room, quietly closing the door behind her. It was then that I could distinctly follow Billy's end of the phone conversation.

"Yeah, we've got the surveillance tapes all ready. I know. You can have them when you want 'em. Yeah, she's sitting right here. What? You're kidding me."

My heart started thudding. Was that Mr. Smarty-pants DEA? Oh my gosh, was he already telling Billy what I had been doing? There is no honor among thieves or DEA agents, either. I might as well get up and walk out right now. Billy was looking at me with a ...What look was that? Disgust? Fury? Puzzlement?

I gathered up all my papers from my lap and started to rise. Billy motioned me to sit back down with his free hand. The other conversationalist had continued to talk all this time. If this dialogue was about me and my latest antics, there was surely a lot to say ... a lot more than I had actually done. I started formulating some excuses in my head.

Let's see, according to my time frame, I couldn't have done all the things the caller said because there simply were not enough hours in the day. And Steve could testify to the fact that I had been at the office all night, well almost all night. The kids could, too. I envisioned the character witnesses I could call. One, two, okay maybe not two, but I could surely find one character witness. Now what was he saying?

"Oh, I wouldn't go so far as that. Sure, she's annoying, but she means well. Yeah, I know him, too. Really? He usually keeps his nose clean."

Oh, now really! Did they have to blame me for Steve's actions, too? Wasn't it enough that I was going to be in trouble for my own behavior?

"Well, I can handle her. Yep. Got it covered. Talk to you later."

Billy reached over to the phone cradle and put the hand set in slowly. It was the effort of a tired and exhausted man. I immediately felt remorseful and could feel my anger at being discussed like a disobedient child give way to my concern for him.

"So, Kid, whatcha got?"

"Well, these …," papers slid into the floor and flooded onto his desk as I stood to show him what I had. I started to go through them. "Oh, sorry. Look, let me just tell you what's happened then you can decide what you need to see." And then, I couldn't contain myself any longer.

"Who was that on the phone?"

"Why?"

"I …it sounded like you were …talking …about me."

"We were."

"So, who was it?"

"Who do you think it was?"

"Uh-Uh. I'm not falling into that trap."

"Have you been doing something you shouldn't?"

"What makes you ask that?"

"Because you look as guilty as Senator Hughes."

"That's what I want to talk to you about."

"I know."

"You know?"

"Yeah."

"You mean you know Senator Hughes and Garth Miller own property at the industrial park, that Garth and Harvey Layfield were using it as a drug trafficking site? And you know Senator Hughes was helping Garth get his senatorial seat because Garth was paying him to? And you know that Harvey Layfield was out in Vegas at least ten times this year and owed huge gambling debts? And you know that ..." I stopped short of the next one because I wasn't sure if, even I, knew that one.

"Well, I didn't know all of that, but I'm assuming you came to tell me because that was Steve on the phone and he told me basically what you just said, and that you two are putting together the front page. He says to hurry up, that you have work to do."

"Oh my gosh! I forgot. I have to go and type my stories," I said as I rose to go.

"Wait, Mibbie, what did you want to show me?"

"Oh, right. Well, look, here is a timeline." I sifted through the papers and found the chart I had constructed. I handed it to him. "Here is the evidence." I swept my hand over all the papers scattered on his desk and on the floor. I stooped over to get the rest.

Billy smiled as he took my piece of legal pad paper. He

scanned it, then examined the jumbled mess of copies I had picked up off the floor and placed on the desk with the others.

He looked up from them, and said, "Good work, Mibbie. Did you do anything illegal to get this stuff?"

"Is it illegal to sort through a drunk man's papers?"

"Was he there?"

"Yes."

"Did he give you permission to do it and to make these copies?"

"Um. Yes."

"You hesitated."

"No, I have it on tape. I asked and he said 'yes.'"

"Well, a good defense attorney will claim that his inebriated state lacked the proper consent, but other than that, it sounds like you did everything by the book, which will matter when we take this to court for prosecution. Did you stop by the District Attorney's office with this?"

"Uh-Uh. Came straight here. Well, straight here after I went to see Senator Hughes to confirm some of the facts. I wanted it to be right for my story."

"Alright, I'll contact the DA. The sooner he gets his hands on the evidence the better. Also, we don't want any of the witnesses disappearing on us. Rumor has it that the city police chief is missing. I'll call Judge Tarleton and get some search warrants pulled together. Anything else?"

"Nope. Not a thing. That's it. Right here." I patted the papers.

"Mibbie?"

"No, that's it."

"Mibbie?"

"Okay, there is one more thing, but I am confirming it. As soon as I am positive, I will bring you the evidence, alright?"

Billy smiled. It was a weary I-know-what -you are-up-to-smile. "Okay, Kid. Keep your nose clean."

It felt good to have him return to normal with me. I stood up to go.

"Billy?"

"Yeah?"

"You really are a good cop."

"Thanks Mibbie, you're a good reporter."

I bounded out of his office and back to mine. Steve was pacing the floor.

"Where have you been?"

"Now, that's a silly question. You know perfectly well where I've been. You just talked to Billy. And by the way, what's this business about scooping me? I wanted to tell him myself."

"C'mon, we don't have time for your vanity."

"Oh, right, we have time for yours, but ..." Steve grabbed my arm and pulled me over to my computer. "Type," he commanded, and shoved me into my chair.

So, I got started. There comes a point when you have been up all night that it ceases to matter. Your body has this miraculous way of coping without any sleep and functioning anyway. Steve had made a pot of coffee while I had gone to see Billy and Gladys had picked up some breakfast sandwiches from the deli. This was uncharacteristic of her, so I suspected Steve had forced her into being thoughtful. That meant I was going to be working through breakfast, lunch, and if I didn't finish my stories, dinner, also.

Steve had already done the headlines and cropped the pictures. That was a huge time-saving help. All I had to do was concentrate on the tag lines for the pictures and the copy for the stories. Since I had been over the facts once with Harvey, in finding everything out in the first place, rehearsed it with the Senator, then back over the same ground again with Billy, I found the words flowing freely. Steve had done a side-by-side of Garth's murder, so mine fit in nicely explaining the connection with Senator Hughes as a possible explanation without saying too much, and offending the DEA agent.

Billy had saved me time by contacting the District Attorney's office to tell them how much would appear in the paper. The DA had called Steve and asked for no mention to be made of the drug connection, but everything else was fair game; he hoped the story in *The World* would prompt a feeding frenzy of people who knew what was going on, or at least, thought they did, and would provide fruit-yielding leads. We were to refer to the contents of the trucks as "unauthorized transport goods."

Normally, Steve would have balked at such an order, but his secret knowledge of the actual content of the trucks combined with his pictures of the trucks at the industrial park and his assurance from the DEA agent that another story would be forthcoming made him less polemic. Right now, the story of the day was political corruption and Garth's murder.

I dodged between my taped conversation with Senator Hughes and my notes from the night before. Pretty soon, I had three stories that were lucid: "Industrial Park Object of Investigation"; "Senator and Mayor Involved in Trucking Scam"; " Local Car Dealer Faces Gambling Charges." Combined with Steve's story on Garth's murder, I thought this front page was the best one we'd ever had. The hard part about being a reporter is that it is addictive to have your name in print, and the front page is the "meth" of the newspaper trade. It is exhilarating and empowering. This edition was a terrific one and would only make us work harder next week.

They say when you are in the newspaper business, you bleed ink; I could believe it. As determined as I was to get these stories front page worthy, I kept an eye on the clock. The only thing that would tear me away from this very exciting newspaper moment was my children.

Even though they are 18 and 16, leaving my children alone all night had been unconscionable, and I needed to get back to them with an explanation and an apology. I felt myself pulled into reading and re-reading the text time and time again. I wanted it to be perfect.

It was 3:10, just time enough to leave the office and get home before the girls did. When I shoved back my chair and reached for my purse, Steve, who was standing over me reading the copy I had just printed out for the third time, looked shocked.

"Hey, where are you going?"

"Steve, it's good. We have a near-perfect front page. I've checked it and rechecked it. It's good. I need to go home and make amends with my kids."

"Mibbie..."

"No, Steve, I'm going to go. By my count, I've already put in forty hours and we aren't even halfway through the week. I'm going home. If you need to change something, you have my permission to do it. I've been up all night and my kids need me."

I picked up my purse, aware for the first time today just how spent I really was. When Steve grabbed my arm, I thought I might punch him in the nose.

"Mibbie, take tomorrow off."

"What?"

"You deserve it. You're right. You've put in enough time. Take tomorrow off."

I wasn't sure if I was going to faint because my physical frame was giving out or because Steve had said the most incredible thing I had ever heard him say.

"Gee, thanks," was all I could manage.

Chapter 28

Mechanical action took over and I found myself driving through our little town on familiar roads. Morton looked so innocent and unaware in the late afternoon spring light. Everything was "new green", that nearly transparent hue you see for only a brief time before the emerald-green of full bloom sets in. I remembered seeing that color in my 64-count box of Crayola Crayons when I was in elementary school, and wondering why it was called that. It's lovely becoming an adult and having childhood questions answered.

I loved driving into the driveway and seeing the children's cars parked there: everybody home, everybody safe.

It was disbelief I saw on my children's faces when I walked through the door at 4:00 P.M. instead of 6:30 or 8:00 P.M. The astonishment swiftly changed to anger, though, when the girls recalled why their brother was home for dinner. I held my hand up in the defensive mode.

"Tell you what, guys, let's make some dinner, then we'll sit down to eat and I'll tell you all about it."

This seemed to pacify them, and we collectively started pulling ingredients out of the cabinets and the refrigerator. The next thirty minutes was a pageantry of teamwork as one boiled water and cooked pasta, another braised asparagus and one more braised Italian sausage all in the small space of our kitchen. I set the table and made the tea, filling the glasses with ice and the dishwasher with soap for the after-dinner dishes.

When we sat down later, I was so happy to have my whole brood once more gathered around the table, I almost forgot my original mission. Their looks of anticipation got me back on track. Here was their reaction to my most egregious act: going into our local dive that only the dregs of our community frequent:

"You went to The Blue Moon? Cool!"

"I am going to be so embarrassed if anybody finds out what you've done."

"So, does this mean we can go there, too?"

I sat back and smiled a very satisfied smile. It was one of those Emerson moments: "God is in His heaven and all's right with the world." My son would set his alarm early and drive back to college for classes. But for tonight, we were all together in our usual places, around the table. They put in a movie and woke me fifteen minutes into it to tell me I should go upstairs to bed, that I had already fallen asleep.

Chapter 29

The next morning, the children tried awfully hard to be quiet. They would have done an admirable job for anyone other than their mother. I have what I call "Mother Ears" which means I hear everything in the house pertaining to my children.

I heard my son's alarm go off and him rustling out of the bed. I heard him make coffee downstairs and run the shower. I started to get up to steal another kiss from him before saying goodbye, but I knew he would be distressed at having awoken me. I heard him start his jeep and set out for college. An hour later two more alarms went off and two girls performed the same routine.

I tried to sleep a while after they were gone, but I'm not much on sleeping in. I wake up early on my own, and the most delicious thing in the world is to have a whole day stretch out in front of you with nothing demanding or compelling to do. Sleeping seemed like a waste.

This was a morning for an omelet breakfast, complete with crunchy bell peppers, rich Virginia ham, sharp cheddar cheese and thick sour cream. It was a morning for coffee with cream, sipped on the front porch swing, drunk leisurely, instead of hurriedly gulping it down before practically throwing the mug in the sink in a hurry to head out for work.

There was time to look at a magazine while swinging

lazily in the hammock and watching the sun shift in patterns across the yard. It was going to be a glorious day with blue skies and one or two puffs of clouds floating by on their way to a party in the mountains. And that is exactly how I spent the first few hours of my precious day off. But as with all things luxurious and wonderful, it had to come to an end.

I heard that annoying whining of a motorized vehicle out in the woods, the one that sounds like the buzz of a mosquito next to your ear and drives you nearly insane with its incessant whirring. Also known as ATV's (all-terrain vehicles), we'd had trouble with four-wheelers racing up and down the quiet road and the power line near the house. The power company erected an iron gate to prevent that.

The woods and secluded roads are intersected by a power line that connects to another road further down, so it is possible to gain access without having to come down my road and being deterred from getting on the power line by the gate. While the offending creatures had found another route, at least the racing had been inhibited, and the four wheelers were discouraged from coming this direction. The main road leading past my house was quiet once more.

Unfortunately, another problem we had were hunters, who would ride their four-wheelers out to target practice on the power line without fear of being accosted by the game warden for a hunting license. In the fall, their bullets would zing past our heads when we hiked. I feared for the fawn colored boxer I had. He was just the right color to be mistaken for a deer.

Hearing the four-wheelers now, I realized now that their

presence had been in my subconscious for some time. I had heard them at night a couple of weeks ago, and was now hearing them during the day in the middle of the week when John Q. Citizen would normally be at work.

Before, I had other things taxing my time, but now I could do something about it. I could hike out, try to talk some sense into them, and short of that, at least take down names and report them. Since it was spring, I was less worried about hunters, who might mistake one of my dogs for a deer, or me for a wild boar.

If they were just kids skipping school and looking for something to do, my mere presence would be enough to spook them into not doing this again.

The dogs were excited the minute I pulled out my dusty boots. They knew what that meant, in the same way they knew what the clinking of their leashes meant. I set out from my house and headed up the paved road I live on to the power line road about half a mile away. I could hear four wheelers as I approached, but I couldn't see them. I checked my pocket for my cell phone. If I couldn't convince the deviants to amend their ways, I could take pictures and give them to Billy. While it didn't work at my house, my cell phone had service on the power line.

I began walking at a clipped pace, and the dogs followed in suit, but the four- wheelers eluded me. I had gone about two miles on the power line, but still no sign of the lawless pack. Sound carries far out in the country, with nothing to obstruct it, and the noise of a thing can come from one direction when, in fact, it might be in a completely different one altogether. Maybe I had been wrong about where the four wheelers were, and where they were headed.

My lungs were arguing vehemently that they were still not in good shape from being sick and needed a rest, but I sensed if I pressed on, I might catch up to the noisemakers eventually. Darn my sense of commitment!

By now, we had walked a total of three miles from home, or so I judged, and I could no longer even hear the four-wheelers. I wished I had thought to bring along some water; I decided to rest on a fallen tree. The terrain was rough and I marveled at the little vehicles that could master it. The day had grown warm and wildlife was showing itself. I watched a hawk circling above and was caught by surprise when two deer stepped tentatively into the clearing below. I watched them sense my presence, but still search for me, so I kept the dogs quiet beside me. Even though my errand had been an unpleasant one, it had ended well enough, enjoying the beautiful natural surroundings.

When I regained my strength, I started back over the rise returning on the path I had come. I wasn't so spent yet that I was marking time watching my feet. When I get really tired, I don't have the energy to marvel at the world around me. I just march by looking at one foot going in front of the other. My rest had given me the reserve I needed to enjoy the view. I scanned the area for more signs of wildlife, but it wasn't something wild that caught my eye.

A big box came into view over the second rise, ensconced in some trees. I had missed it on the way up, and even though I had walked this far up here and back before, lots of times, I didn't remember seeing it. Surely, my over-curious nature would have taken note of such an unnatural sight. I hiked over to the box, which turned out to be not a box at all, but a freezer that had been spray-painted to conceal it in the brush.

Of course, I looked inside.

I may have gotten myself in trouble with my overdeveloped sense of curiosity in the past, and I was working on changing my aberrant nature, but it was going to be a slow process.

Drugs.

They weren't concealed in any way. Bold as brass, they sat there waiting for the guy who was going to pick them up. Another four-wheeler guy no doubt. Oh yes, I could have stayed there and waited. I could have tried to do surveillance from a near-by thatch of bushes. I could have tried to redeem myself with news that would make Billy forgive my past transgressions in an instant, but such thoughts and actions were the exact reason why he had gotten mad at me before. Besides, I had proved beyond a shadow of a doubt that I was an incompetent surveillance investigator and that I was ill-equipped to deal with the criminal element.

Billy's severe reprimand from my Corn Dog experience and the experience he still didn't know about yet at the industrial park had trained me well; I didn't touch the drugs; I didn't try to get them out; I didn't try any more to follow the four wheelers, or look around for other evidence. I dialed the sheriff's office.

"Shurff's offs," came the voice from the pit of Hades.

What was I going to do now?

"Shurff's offs," he said louder with a tinge of anger this time. Could I play that my cell phone wasn't working? If I hung up and tried again, I would probably just get Bruce. Best to forge ahead.

"Is Gale in?"

"Naw."

"Billy?"

"Uh-uh."

Well, so much for trying. I pushed the "off" button. Then I had another idea and pushed another set of numbers.

"Steve?"

"Mibbie? Aren't you supposed to be asleep or something?"

"I was. Steve, this has been a great day, thank you, but I need a favor. You know that DEA agent we've been working with?"

"Working with? You mean the one that owes us a story and tried to muscle us out of the industrial park?"

"Yeah, that one. Do you have his number?"

"Why do you want his number?"

Now, here is where it got tricky. If I told him the real reason, he'd be over here in a minute and I'd be put to work. Even with this exciting news, I still didn't want to give up my vacation day. I nurtured fond hopes of a well-prepared lunch instead of fast food, and a decent dinner for my ever-patient daughters. So, I had to think of something quick, and it had to be plausible.

"I wanted to ask him out," I blurted out.

I closed my eyes and squished up my face preparing for what was coming next. At first it was silence, then it was a burst of laughter.

"You want to ask him out?" Steve asked in between his howls of laughter.

"Yeah, you know … I was enjoying my day and I just thought, …he might… you know, like … to go out or something."

"You want to ask him out." It was a statement this time.

"Do you think I shouldn't? You think he won't go? What?"

"No. No. You want to ask him out?"

"Steve, what? Are you baffled? Are you amused? Will you stop humiliating me and just give me the number?"

"Sure, sure. Hold on while I go get his card."

He came back on the line a minute later and read the numbers off to me very slowly like I might not have the mental capacity to understand digits. I permitted this undue teasing.

"Okay, thanks. I'll see you tomorrow."

"Mibbie?"

"Yeah, Steve?"

"If he says 'no' you can always ask me out."

"Oh very funny, boss man. I don't know if I can stand it."

His laughter was still ringing in my ears when I looked at the number now highlighted on my phone. Here goes.

Chapter 30

I was thankful when he answered on the third ring.

"Agent Dees."

"Agent Dees? (Did I sound ridiculous restating his name?) This is Mibbie Wright. We met yesterday at the industrial park. Well, actually we've sort of met before, um, when I went to one of our local restaurants. We didn't actually meet, then, but you knew about me, and it isn't really a restaurant. Um, not anymore, you know because The Corn Dog doesn't really exist. But you might remember me from yesterday. I was …"

"I remember," but then he was silent, and I had to speak again.

"I'm calling because I found something and I needed to tell someone."

"Okay."

"You're not going to make this easy are you? Look, I'm out on my power line and I found what I think is a drop-off for drugs. Some four-wheeler riders were here and I think they dropped them off. I called the sheriff, but …" Should I tell him that I didn't get to talk to Billy because my arch-enemy answered the phone, and I didn't leave a message because I was worried about corruption in the Sheriff's Department? No, that would make me sound insane, and I thought Agent Dees might consider me certifiable already.

185

"Yes?"

"Well, I found these drugs and I thought someone should know."

"Are you standing beside them?"

"Yes."

"Don't you think someone is watching you?"

"No. I mean, I don't think so. The people who dropped them off are long gone. I wouldn't think the people who are going to pick them up would be that close by now. What would be the point of having a drop-off if you could just hand them off to someone."

"Have you been in the drug trade very long?"

"No. Wait … I've never been in the drug trade. No, I'm not the drug runner. These aren't my drugs. I didn't …"

"Oh, don't worry, I figured that out already. You aren't the world's smartest criminal."

"Hey!"

"Okay, just listen. Here is Drug Running 101. You never keep the drugs in your possession. Dump them as quickly as possible. If you aren't holding, no one can arrest you for it. So, it makes sense that your four wheeling drug runners dumped them, but that doesn't mean the other couriers aren't nearby ready to pick them up.

"Now, *you* stumble onto the scene and they see you standing there beside their drugs with a phone in your hand. Since you don't look like a criminal, they know you're not there for the drugs. I'm assuming you're not doing the drugs, so recreational use is also out. That means you are probably a do-good citizen who is calling the authorities, which you are.

"So, they will do one of two things," he continued. "Either they will kill you, or they will scram and I have just had another monkey wrench thrown into my case.

"By the way, are you trying to ruin this case for me?" he added. "Are you trying to sabotage my chances for promotion? Because if you are, it would be a lot easier if I just stop working, than to do all of this investigating just to have you come along and blow it."

"Did you say, 'Kill me?'" I asked incredulously.

"Yeah, but you're not dead yet, so my bet is on the scram."

"Yes, but you said 'Kill me.'"

"I did, but I'm still talking to you, so they aren't going to kill you. Nope, you've just made my job a lot harder."

"I'm sorry," I said.

"I know. You always are. Every time you have botched up my case you have said you are sorry. So, I'll tell you what. Hang up the phone and walk away from those drugs. I'm assuming you have a vehicle nearby."

"No, I walked."

"What?"

"I walked. I live near here."

"Oh, this is just great. All right, now listen. Are you in a place where I can get to you?"

"No. I'm on the power line."

"What are you doing on a power line? No, never mind that, just get to a place where I can get to you the easiest. Stay put. Do not go home. I repeat. Do not go home. When you get to the place where I can get to you. Stop. Call me. Do not go anywhere else."

"Wouldn't it make more sense for me to tell you where I am, so you can come here, then I can watch the drugs and you can meet me and it will save ti..."

"You don't take orders very well, do you?" Agent Dees cut in. "Will you try to trust the professionals? I do this for a living. Now WILL YOU GET OFF THE PHONE?!?!?!?"

I pushed the "off" button, and started one of those long walks. You know the kind. The one where you have just tripped and fallen on the stage in front of the whole student body, and they are all laughing, and you have to get up and walk across the rest of the stage, anyway. Only in this case, I wasn't sure if the whole student body wasn't pointing a gun at me instead of laughing at me.

They say dogs sense fear. Mine just trotted happily along beside me, oblivious to my emotional tornado, or any of the desperadoes who might be lurking in the woods waiting to take me out. Well done, faithful canines.

Chapter 31

I sat on the side of the road, after calling Agent Dees with my location, really wishing I had brought water, waiting for a man who was going to scold me. At least when it was my dad, I knew he loved me. This guy just seemed to want to humble me. Even though the road I live on stretches about two miles to the next road attached to it, you can hear vehicles coming from far away.

So, I knew the car that was approaching was probably Agent Dees. I considered running away, but if he was right about the criminals now inhabiting my woods, I wasn't going to be safe at home and worse, I would endanger my girls. His scolding would be worth it to keep them safe.

Most law enforcement vehicles look alike. That's why you can spot an unmarked traffic cop lurking in the trees, or on the side of the road, waiting to catch the heedless speeder. So, when the sedan came into sight, I was sure that it was Agent Dees behind the wheel.

He got out of the car dressed in office attire, clean white shirt, tie and suit, but quickly slipped out of his loafers into hiking boots, and out of his jacket into a windbreaker. He took out two bottles of water. One, he put in his backpack, the other he gave to me. I was so grateful I drained the bottle at that very moment.

"Thank you," I said.

He didn't say anything, just gave me a "forward" motion with his upturned hand. I lead the way back up the steep incline of the power line and onto the path made in the high grass over the hills and valleys. We didn't speak the whole way.

In my "encyclopedia of male behavior" that silence meant we were about business and words were unnecessary. I learned this bit of wisdom by watching *The Magnificent Seven* with Yul Brynner. It is the icon of male movies, unless you count Clint Eastwood's spaghetti westerns. To indicate he should go after the bad guys, Yul Brynner motions to James Coburn with a nod of his head. When Charles Bronson reports on how many there were and how many are dead, he does so with a thumbs up and a thumbs down. No words; just motions. And the men understand the motions. Women who pay attention to these cinematic samples and their subtle messages will learn the language of the silent male.

When we got to the box, Agent Dees unloaded his backpack of equipment. He took pictures, pulled on rubber gloves and examined the contents of the drug packages. He dusted for fingerprints, pausing to look at me with disgust.

I am sure my face gave away that, "Yes, I have touched that box and lifted the lid, so I probably smudged some really important prints." I didn't say anything though, and directed the fullness of my attention to what he was doing as if I were the most innocent creature in the world. He wiped the box lid down when he had finished and stuffed all of his equipment back into his backpack.

We had still not spoken, and I thought he might be about to say something, but I was wrong. This time, I didn't even get a hand signal. He cocked his head to one side and raised his eyebrows and pursed his lips with a "Let's go" facial expression. It looked like I was losing even the little communication I had going for me. We started out once more, trekking along in silence, until we reached his car. He sat down in his back seat to exchange his boots for his shoes, and finally spoke.

"How far from here do you live?"

I pointed back down the road from which he had come an hour ago. "That way, about half a mile."

"Alright, see you later."

"You mean you're not going to offer me a ride?"

"It's not that far."

"I just walked that stretch behind us ... twice. No, ordinarily it wouldn't be that far, but right now it is, and besides, didn't your mama teach you it is bad manners not to offer a lady a ride and see her safely home, especially since we just went back to the place you told me to leave because it was likely I was being watched, and I might even get killed."

"I was just kidding about that. Yeah, you're right, climb in."

But now, I was indignant, and my feminine pride took over.

"Kidding. Do you think that is funny? I live out here, and I have children. Threats to our lives are not funny. No, thank you, I can walk by myself. I hope I do get killed, because then you can get your stupid promotion solving my murder."

I turned on my furious heel and stalked down the road toward the house as well as a very tired and sore woman of a certain age can stalk. He coasted his car up beside me a minute later. I kept walking, refusing to look at him.

"Ah c'mon, it was a joke. Get in," he said as he rolled along beside me.

"No, thank you."

"Can't you take a joke? Get in."

"I would rather walk with my dogs than ride with a rude man."

He pulled his car to an angle in front of me and stopped. I started to walk around it. He got out and locked it, then sauntered up beside me.

"Worried about car thieves?" I snapped at him tartly.

"You didn't have any brothers did you?"

"What does my family composite have to do with anything?"

"If you'd had brothers, you would be used to teasing and you wouldn't have taken this so personally."

"And what makes you think that your disrespectful behavior could somehow resemble familial playfulness, particularly since we hardly know each other." To put psychological evidence of my anger in my body language, I crossed my arms and huffed.

"Let's just say I got it wrong and I'm trying to make it up to you. Will you please get in the car?"

"No."

"Look, I said I was sorry."

"You did? Because I do not recall hearing *those* words come from *your* lips." I pointed at his face as I said it. "Hmmm. Thinking." I tapped my head to emphasize I was carefully remembering. "Nope. No 'I'm sorry' was forthcoming."

"Okay, you're right. I did not say those words. I had no idea you were so literal, but yeah, okay, here goes: I'm sorry. Better now?"

I thought a little more time before answering would make my point clearer.

"I'm sorry? That's it? I'm not sure those words are sufficient. I seem to recall you saying that my own 'I'm sorry' was quite inadequate."

"You know what? You got me again. I did say that. Well, not exactly that, but you're right. I'm not just sorry. I really regret that I teased you in a way that made you angry and sounded insensitive about your welfare."

I was taken aback, as I am sure my shocked expression indicated. I had to admit, *that* was a good apology. I sighed heavily and said, "Alright, fine."

As we approached the car, I asked, "Why did you lock your doors?"

"In case you were one of those stubborn women and you decided to keep walking, I was going to walk with you."

I smiled. That was funny. He had disarmed me.

I showed him the driveway to my house, and had an idea I should ask him in for lunch, but it had been a long day and a long time since I had been alone with a man, drunken

Harvey aside, and I didn't think I felt up to the stress. He deposited me on my porch and left.

The rest of my day went as I expected, a nice lunch, a quiet rest swinging in the hammock and intermittently reading my library book. Dinner preparations were finished just as the girls arrived from school. Barbeque chicken and macaroni and cheese, with a side dish of spanakopita (Greek spinach pie), set us up nicely. I was in the mood for Yul Brynner that night. Wonder why?

Chapter 32

The next morning, the phone rang early. Those kinds of phone calls, like late night ones, startle and concern me. It was Billy.

"Hey, Kid. Can you get by the office on your way in today? I think we have something for you."

"Sure." I said, resisting the urge to ask who "we" was. Suddenly I had the unshakeable desire to change my clothes. I had already pulled on a pair of khakis, but decided that I'd change into something a little more feminine. I pulled out a skirt and a collared blouse with a frill down the front. No, too obvious. Knit shirt and small heels.

The heightened interest in my appearance was a little unsettling. I blushed at my reflection as I paused to straighten my skirt and take an appraisal on my way out the door.

Spring was in the air. Everything smelled fresh and new, and it gave me a light step. I wondered if I should call Steve and tell him I'd be in after my visit, but decided against it since he might just want to be there with me. Was I feeling a little giddy?

I sang all the way to Billy's office. Pulling into a parking place, I pushed my sunglasses up on top of my head. Then I looked in the mirror to see the effect. Oh, this was not good: twice to the mirror. The next thing you knew I would be seeing Narcissus on a regular basis. I stepped out of the car and headed up the sidewalk to the front door of the Sheriff's Department. I pretended when I twisted my ankle that I was just adjusting the strap on my shoe. Clearly, I should not be trying to play the coquette. I was not in possession of my right mind.

"Hi honey," Gayle said when I presented myself to the front desk. "Go on b...Well, now." She smiled as she looked me up and down. "Don't we look smart today?"

"Oh, I have to appear in court later," I said, realizing I had materialized my unconscious thoughts.

Gayle was a true friend and did not seek to embarrass me further. "You look really pretty."

I contemplated going home to change, but it was too late for that. I went down the hall feeling like a felon on his way to the electric chair. I noticed my hand was trembling as I reached for the door handle. Great! I could take on gang members, a corrupt Senator and drug couriers, but I could not handle the tiniest bit of male attention.

Besides, I didn't even know if Agent Dees was married, if he had a fiancé, a girlfriend, or what today's youth termed "friends with benefits," a most unflattering position if you asked me, lacking unilateral equality and certainly not something I wanted to be a party to.

I opened the door hesitantly. I could feel my blood pressure rise with the beating of my heart. Good gracious! What was happening to me? This wasn't a job interview, or a public speaking engagement in front of thousands of people, but the pounding of my heart made me feel like I was involved in a plot to overtake a small regime. This was just a meeting in Billy's office where I'd been a thousand times.

Billy's face was the first one I saw as I swung open the door, and in his usual gentlemanly way, he stood up and said, "Here she is. Mibbie Wright, I'd like for you to meet ..." and just then I stumbled on my strappy heels and fell into the filing cabinet next to the door. At least I didn't fall into the floor.

There was no need for all the peremptory strain. The person for whom all that anxiety was building wasn't even there. The only person I actually met was the Lieutenant Governor, who was there for damage control over Senator Hughes and the soon-to-be-vacant senate seat. I'm sure he was disconcerted that any trust would be placed in a person with so little ability to walk into a room.

The other people in the room were: Melvin Collins, the District Attorney, and Judge Tarleton, but I had a long history with both. The men were profusely concerned about my well-being, much to my chagrin, but I managed to laugh and say of my embarrassing fall, "My mama taught me to always make an entrance." As long as you can laugh at yourself, my daddy would tell me, no one can laugh at you.

I should have been honored to be in a meeting like that. It showed how much Billy trusted me to make me privy to the mechanics of this web. As it was, I was busy trying to recover from my mortification and from the humiliation of being eyed carefully by both Billy and Judge Tarleton. I suppose Melvin didn't know me well enough to know that today's outfit marked a tremendous transformation from my usual garment selection.

Both Judge Tarleton and Billy were demonstratively surprised by my new persona. Judge Tarleton kept lifting his eyebrows simultaneously and giving me the "va-va-voom" grin. Billy just looked puzzled. I knew I would be in for an inquisition when the other two men left.

The Lieutenant Governor spoke first. "So, we know that Senator Hughes has resigned his seat effective today. As to who will fill the position, the Governor has not come to a conclusive decision. He has had five names submitted to him for approval. Since this is an election year, the matter is not one of gravity, but we certainly don't want to lose the trust of the people in their elected officials. The vacated seat can be filled by anyone who demonstrates credibility and veracity.

"That person will either be elected in the fall and learn how things work in Montgomery, or someone else will. At any rate, that's only six months away. I would say, I don't think whomever the Governor chooses can do much damage in that length of time, but I may be proved wrong." The Lieutenant Governor looked grim.

"There isn't too much mischief the Governor's choice can get into if we clean up like we think we will," said Melvin.

"I hope that's true," said the Lieutenant Governor.

"We don't have that much going on here," said Judge Tarleton. "I think that's why the Senator and Garth were able to get away with as much as they did. No one would believe such a thing could happen here."

The Lieutenant Governor rose, and for the first time I noticed his bodyguards who had discreetly blended into the wall in the back of the room. They shifted forward so as to precede him out the door. Great! Just what I needed: more witnesses to my incapacity to enter a room without crashing to the floor.

I noticed Billy hadn't said anything, and I wondered why. I hoped I hadn't arrived too late to defend him from being called incompetent by a politician. As a rule I don't care for politicians. They like to point fingers and place blame on others to keep themselves safe from the light of truth. From the Lieutenant Governor's comments, it sounded like we were a bunch of hoodlums who couldn't keep ourselves on the right side of the law, and we had made a mess he'd had to come up here and clean up.

The men all rose and shook hands with one another. I joined in, though I wasn't sure I deserved to. Melvin followed the Lieutenant Governor and his men out.

"Probably going to speak to him about his name being on that short list," said Judge Tarleton.

"That'd be okay," said Billy. "He's done a good job for us. I don't mind an honest man putting himself forward if he deserves to."

Judge Tarleton patted Billy on the back. "You're right, son. I didn't mean to sound ungenerous. Have you told Mibbie about her treat?"

"Not yet," said Billy. "First, I need to find out where she's going. I don't think she'd want to go looking like that."

"And speaking of looking like that …what's up? Were

you trying to impress the big brass? 'Cause if you were, you sure did it," Judge Tarleton said with a grin.

"With the way I look or how I so gracefully entered the room?" I said off-handedly, eager to get the attention off the fact I had dressed for someone who wasn't even here.

"You look beautiful, Kid," said Billy. Honestly, that man is a saint. He had not only paid me a compliment, he had taken some of the sting out of my wounded pride.

"I think the L.G. 's bodyguards thought you meant to do him harm. Did you see them reach for their weapons?" the Judge chuckled quietly.

"Okay, I know you couldn't help that remark. Enough teasing. Can't you see how embarrassed I am?" I felt like climbing under something and hiding.

"Sorry, honey. You look terrific, but Billy's right. You can't go where we're going dressed like that."

"Well, where are we going? A pig sty, barbecue rib eating contest or a garbage dump?"

"You've been in the newspaper business too long if you think those are your only options. Billy, we've got to talk to Steve into getting her better story lines," said the Judge. "I'll let Billy tell you. Meet you at the airport," he said to me as he stood up and headed for the door.

"Airport?" I asked, turning to look at Billy as the Judge made his way out of the office. "Are you going somewhere?"

"We are."

"Who is 'we'?" I asked, being overly cautious since my earlier miscalculation in assuming who "we" might mean.

"You, me and the Judge, that is, if Steve can spare you.

By the way, were you going somewhere? You don't usually dress like this."

"No," I sighed. "You're right; I don't usually dress like this. It was a momentary lapse of my good fashion judgment. I can go and change, if you'll tell me how I should dress."

"You still haven't answered my question."

"Billy, it's called 'avoidance,' and don't tell me Melba hasn't used this technique before when she doesn't want to discuss something that is unpleasant."

"Well, she tells me whatever is going on. If she dressed up, I think I'd know why. If I didn't know why, I'd ask her, and she'd just tell me."

"Such is the life of a happily married couple. My life is a little more complicated."

"Maybe you should try simplifying it," he said. "You'll want your jeans and a sweater and some shoes that don't have heels on them. Do you want to go home now and change? I can meet you at the airport with the Judge, or I can wait for you here."

I like that Billy is the kind of man he is, discretion being one of his many outstanding qualities. He let the fashion matter drop.

"Don't wait for me; I should be back in thirty minutes, but you can get other things done in that time. I'll meet you at the airport." The clothes I had tossed on the bed this morning after I had decided to change were still there, and it would take me all of five minutes to throw them back on and be rid of my ridiculous attempt at allurement. Khakis were as good a substitute for jeans. I thought about what I should say to Steve. If he knew I was headed out for an exciting trip in an airplane, he'd want to go. I pushed the numbers on my cell phone as I walked to the car.

"*The World,*" sang out Gladys.

"Hi, Gladys, it's Mibbie. Is Steve in?"

"No, he's gone to get the last of the information he needs for his story from that city police officer."

This actually was to my benefit. I could leave a message with Gladys that Steve would spend the better part of the morning trying to decipher, by which time I would be back and could explain my absence without his interference. I made the message longer than it had to be, knowing Gladys would have a hard time keeping up and wouldn't be able to get it all. I still had seven months left in the year before Christmas when I'd have to worry about making things right with Santa Claus.

"Would you tell him that Billy called me this morning and needed me to stop by his office for a meeting? I will be taking notes on that meeting, then getting statements from everyone. After that, I have to run home for a minute, then I'll be back at the office. I can type up the story about this morning's meeting and help him with his story if he needs me to. Did you get all of that?"

"Sure," she said in that gravelly voice of hers.

"Okay, see you later." I hung up, aware that my good behavior meter was going to need to be recalibrated. I recited an old aphorism: "Oh, what a tangled web we weave when first we practice to deceive."

Chapter 33

As I sped down the long road to our tiny little airport, I could feel another heart rate acceleration. This time, however, it was not a sense of foreboding, but of excitement as I wondered what lay in store. Because my daddy had been a pilot, I had always loved to fly.

In my last year of college, I had even dated a pilot who was kind enough to take me on as many flights as he could and even let me fly a helicopter once. He was daring, thrilling and, in the end, incapable of being faithful. All that time soaring had made him unable to keep his feet on the ground. We parted without acrimony. I suppose there was nothing between us anyway, except for our love of flying.

I got out of the car and waved to Billy. He and the Judge were standing beside the Judge's Cessna Skyhawk. He had used his need for travel as an excuse to get his own pilot's license and to invest in a plane. He loved flying, and although anything Billy needed to do fell under the category of police work, and would be covered by the county, Judge Tarleton often offered to fly Billy anywhere he needed to go.

"Do I get to know where we are going?" I asked as I sauntered over, beginning to feel the thrill of take off even before we'd gotten in, and trying hard to control it.

"You know where we're going," Billy said. "At least you know the place. We're headed over your way to see if there is anything suspicious going on in the woods behind your house."

I stopped dead in my tracks. The blood in my veins turned to ice water.

"What do you mean?"

"Agent Dees told me about yesterday, that you and he discovered some drugs over on your power line. He's working with his team on his end of it, and I told him I'd see if we could trace the line of origin. Didn't he tell you?"

"Um, no. He didn't." I paused to see if Billy was angry. I thought he would be, given that I didn't tell him about my escapades on my day off. This wouldn't have been the first time I had concealed something from him that I should have told him. Images of his ferocious face made my throat constrict. Billy continued.

"He didn't tell you we'd be checking on that? That's strange. He was worried about you. Called me yesterday afternoon and wondered if I had a dependable guy who could watch your house. When he told me why, I thought maybe you didn't realize the danger you were in, so I sent Willis over. You know," Billy turned to Judge Tarleton and brushed the judge's upper arm with a flick of the back of his fingers, "this is going to make Willis think he's got some new talent. Mibbie didn't spot him. I'll never get him back on regular duty again."

"He was worried about me?" I knew I sounded too interested in Agent Dees's role in all of this, but I couldn't help it.

"Mibbie, honey," Judge Tarleton scolded, "you don't

play around with drug dealers. Didn't you realize what you'd found?"

"I knew what I'd found. I just didn't realize the ramifications. He called you? He was worried about me?"

Billy turned fully to look at me. "You keep asking that? Why is that so hard to believe?"

"I didn't think he liked me."

Billy asked, "Why would you think that?"

"He ..." Now what was I going to say? "He teased me." "He made fun of me." "He wouldn't talk to me." I could add: "He didn't show up at this morning's meeting." It sounded so juvenile, and I felt juvenile, too, so I erred on the side of caution.

"He has acted as though I have interfered in his investigation."

Both Billy and Judge Tarleton burst out laughing.

"That may be because you keep doing that. We know you. You don't mean to get in the way. That's just your natural curiosity, but he doesn't know that. You know, he's a good cop. He is going to do his job, so if you found something that could be harmful, he is going to do what he can to protect you, even if you are too busy running into trouble to see the danger yourself."

I let my friends have a good laugh at my expense. It was my own fault for trying to act with subterfuge. Did I think I was 007? I was just barely clever enough to be a reporter.

Soon, I was soaring through the sky with Billy and Judge Tarleton over the terrain of our county. Wisps of polluted air rose above our factories in town, forming clouds of their own to mix with the gathering clouds of a late-April storm. Flying through clouds is one of the greatest experiences in the world, unless, of course, you are afraid of flying. Then, it is just terrifying.

Below us, fingers of our county lakes were grasping toward one another over the recreational land that would soon be filled with summer vacationers. The mountains, like wrinkled cotton shirts, gave me the landmark of the area near the interstate. There it was, that death-trap of a roadway, like a mighty python winding its way between the big cities in either direction, sprawling out in the distance.

We were headed for the power line on the road where I lived to see what had lured drug traffickers to the area. It wasn't long before we were above a desolate tract of country, covered by acres of woodlands, but marked by so many dark rust colored scars that I recognized as the Alabama red clay roads. Loggers had carved them out for clear-cutting; hunters and four-wheelers used them, as well as horseback riding clubs. None of this activity was illegal, providing the hunter's licenses were up-to-date and the four wheelers stayed off the power lines and weren't hiding drugs in painted freezers.

That is what made for a perfect cover. If seen from the air, drug couriers looked like any of the thousand law-abiding citizens traversing the mountain. If seen by land, they could easily escape through the maze of twisting roads to the cover of the forest.

About thirty minutes into this kind of scenery, Billy saw it. On top of a mountain's rising hill, with trees cascading down the side of it, lay a small runway, remarkable because it was a paved tarmac instead of the typical red clay strips of road around it. He touched the judge gently on the arm and pointed to it. The judge nodded back to Billy.

Again, like the drop zone I had found earlier the day before, a perfectly concealed hiding place because there was virtually nothing around it: no power lines, no homes, not one fragment of civilization, so no reason for anyone to be in the area, no reason for law enforcement to be hovering around. Even the big airlines passing over it would miss it. You'd only find it if you had years of detective work behind you like Billy did.

Conversation was difficult, but not impossible, with the radio mikes on our ears. We saved words for important things to say. But this revelation only required Billy's forefinger pointing into the distance to reveal what we all knew.

Morton, our innocent little by-way of a town, had become the prime dropping off point for illegal drug activity. It was easy to see why they had chosen it, surrounded as it was by acres of mountains and trees that made for easy natural cover. But it was also well placed because it was perfectly situated between two large cities that would boost the drug trade.

All those customers, and in both directions, and a great way to feed the drug traffic in all the arteries running out of those big cities.

Billy pointed to the navigational map he had stretched out on my lap. I used the highlighter he had given me to mark the longitude and latitude of the runway using the airplane's flying instruments. The judge didn't linger or take time to look really well. He flew north for another twenty minutes or so before arcing back on the return flight, not wanting to alert anyone who might be watching that we had found them.

Once we landed, Billy was all action. It was time for me to keep quiet and out of his way. As I headed for my car to go back to the office, Billy called after me.

"Come over for lunch. Melba says it'll be ready at 12:00."

"I'll be there," I called back.

It felt good to do something so consistent and solid as having lunch with Billy and Melba at their house.

When I opened the back door to the office, I was greeted by an ecstatic editor. Steve had just put the finishing touches on his story about the industrial park being a drug drop spot. He didn't seem to notice I had been incommunicado for a while.

He had seen Agent Dees that morning after his visit to the city police department and convinced him to give over the information he had withheld from us at the great industrial park stakeout. I cringed when he told me this, realizing how Billy must have felt being given this story for the first time. I had hoped to leave that part of my amateur detective foibles out.

"My story on the industrial park will go so well with your story on the drug trafficking going on in your backyard!" Steve enthused.

"I'm not writing that story and you know it. All I need

is for those criminals to figure out that my name is the one on the mailbox next to the power line and they will be shooting at me from the woods," I said hotly.

"Then don't tell the location, but write about the other spot." My hostility to this suggestion had not dampened his excitement at all.

"You know I can't write about what Agent Dees and I found. He let me go along so I could show him the way, not so I could write about it in the newspaper. I can't let him down like that."

But Steve was determined that the drug trafficking angle on the front page from both in the city, and out in the country, was too good a front page to pass up. I decided to appease him by sitting down at my computer and taking out my notebook. He wouldn't know that I wasn't obeying his orders until later. For now, I would type up the story about my meeting this morning, then slip out to Billy and Melba's for lunch. After that, I could figure out what to do next.

Chapter 34

The drive out to Melba and Billy's was as pleasant as a drive home. That is how they always made me feel, like I was coming home. It may sound as if I am envious of their marriage; I'm not. Good marriages are rare, and a gift not everyone gets, but when I see them, I admire them. I am truly grateful there are good marriages in the world as a testimony to the rest of us they can be had.

Billy and Melba lived in a section of our town that could actually be considered rural. It has a row of houses widely spread apart backed up against a small lake, big enough to host a fishing boat or two and plenty big for the fishing Billy does to loosen the tight muscles that come with his job. I fully expected him to be sitting on the small dock below his house when I arrived, but it was empty. I got out of the car and walked toward the deck in the back of the house.

One of the lessons I learned about living in the country part of our little town is that most people do not make use of their front doors. I learned this after going to the wrong door a number of times and the residents of said houses coming from the back to retrieve me and let me know I was knocking on the wrong door. Now I look for telltale signs of foot traffic to determine which door to knock on.

A fluffy cat with languid eyes greeted me from her perch on the railing as I ascended the short staircase. A breeze freshened in the trees and wafted across the shining wood of the deck. Somewhere in the woods across the lake a bird called the cheery greeting of a beautiful day.

I stalled my forward motion for a moment and stopped to feel spring. The sun shone warm and full on a place I knew shortly would be outfitted with chairs and cushions. Spring was such a glorious time filled with hope and promise.

"C'mon in here, girl," said Melba as she exited the glass kitchen door and crossed to enfold me in her arms. She must have been watching for me. "I haven't seen you in a month of Sundays. Billy says you have been up to your usual tricks. When are you ever going to settle down and have a nice, quiet life like the rest of us?"

"You can say that with your husband being the sheriff of this county?" I smiled back at her. I slipped my arm around her waist as she had done hers around mine and we walked like schoolgirls into the house. Billy was at the sink washing his hands.

"Hey, Kid. Hungry? Melba's made a feast even though it's just us."

"And who says you two can't have as much as you want? Last time I checked, neither one of you was eatin' too well, or too much." Somehow she always knew.

The table was set with the food on it, family style. There were hot yeast rolls with butter nearby to slather on, fried chicken dressed up in a caramel brown, crispy coat, fresh green beans cooked to a delicate lime hue and mashed potatoes that looked like the snows of Kilimanjaro. Good food, good friends, and goodness, just plain old-fashioned goodness. It made it easier to come clean about my transgressions.

Over lunch, I explained about the box I had found on the power line and confessed to my attempt at a stakeout at the industrial park.

"Billy," I said. "I really did try to call you first. When Bruce answered, I felt like the next best thing was to call Agent Dees."

"I'm not upset about that," Billy said. "What I'm not happy about is the industrial park. Agent Dees is right, you could have ruined his case. Now, *that* I am upset about, especially since you promised me you wouldn't meddle without my knowing again."

"You are absolutely right. I was just trying to fill in the gaps for our story on Harvey Layfield and the Senator. I should have told you."

"Well, to be honest with you, I already knew. We've been helping Agent Dees with our own stakeout there."

"So, that's how Agent Dees knew Steve and I were there. I wondered about that."

Billy was working "hand in glove" with the DEA, in particular, Rick Dees. Since this was Billy's county, Agent Dees had seen to it that Billy was part of the cleanup of the drug activity. Normally, there is a "squeeze out" of local law enforcement. The DEA likes to work uninhibited, but Agent Dees seemed like a smart man who knew how much help Billy was going to be.

Besides, for Billy, this was personal. Being able to work with Agent Dees was his vindication for Fred getting shot, and the city law enforcement opening the door to crime. If there was anything more despicable to a clean cop than a dirty one I didn't know what it was.

"Honey, is there something else that's been going on?" Melba asked.

"What, besides drugs in my backyard and bullets flying? Isn't that enough?" I winced as I realized I had brought up Fred getting shot again. I gave Billy a sidelong glance to see if he noticed it. He was spooning potatoes onto his plate and didn't look up.

"Well, that is quite enough, but what I wanted to talk to you about is this morning."

"You mean flying over the mountains?" I asked.

"No, a little more personal than that. Billy said you looked really nice this morning, and that you wouldn't tell him why you were so dressed up. You want to talk about it?"

To a stranger listening in, being blindsided like this might seem rude. Other people might be angry to be talked to like this, but when I wouldn't talk to Billy this morning, I knew we'd be having one of these conversations. It wasn't our first one.

Billy and Melba were the closest things I had to siblings. These discussions were to help me over the difficult part of baring my soul, something all humans need to do once in a while. It isn't easy to be a woman alone raising children. You need someone to confide in, to talk to about your own feelings and concerns. As a mother, you hide these things to protect your children. With Billy and Melba, I was safe.

"Okay, I changed up my wardrobe because I was hoping

someone would be at that meeting this morning, who was not, as it turned out."

"Agent Dees?" asked Melba.

"Yes."

"Do you like him?"

"Gosh, Melba, when you say it like that, I sound like a kid in high school."

"Well, honey, there's nothing wrong with an adult having young feelings. It's only wrong if you act like a juvenile when you are supposed to be acting like an adult."

"Then, yes, I think I like him. He was awfully hard on me yesterday. There's something there, maybe chemistry, but I know to be cautious about that. Sometimes chemistry is a dangerous thing."

Melba scooped up some potatoes and took a bite. She was thoughtful for a moment, then said, "You're right. You have to be cautious. You know he called Billy about you yesterday."

"Yes, but only to make sure that his job was being done."

"I don't want to encourage you to do something you shouldn't. I don't know if Agent Dees is a good man. He seems to be. When you say he called Billy to make sure his job was being done, that's a good thing. It's a good quality. Maybe there is nothing more to it than that, but even so, it's a good thing. Don't change anything for him. If he likes you, that will be enough. You're pretty Mibbie. You can dress up when you want, but you don't have to do it for anyone, except you."

"Thanks, Melba."

"Only the very best man deserves you." We both smiled.

Billy was typically quiet in these conversations. He seemed to have an uncanny ability to be in the midst of "girl talk" without making the girls feel concerned about his presence. He reached over and squeezed Melba's hand. They had both made me feel less nervous about this new possibility in my life.

We spent the rest of the hour eating and talking about my children and the upcoming graduation. I jumped up to go when I realized it was 1:30. I kissed Melba and hugged Billy, racing out the door and to my car as quickly as possible. Steve wasn't mad about my long lunch until he realized I hadn't written the story I promised.

"What do you mean you didn't write it?" Steve yelled. "What were you doing before you went to lunch?"

"I have another story for you, but I can't write it, yet. I have to get permission for it from Billy. As soon as I do, you'll be pleased."

"We go to print shortly. Were you planning on having it by then, or did you think we're going to hold the presses for you?"

"Steve, you know good and well that everything we are writing about right now is part of an investigation. And I know you know we are not allowed to jeopardize that investigation just so you can have a front-page story. We had a meeting this morning with the Lieutenant Governor that is certainly front-page worthy. They told me what I could write about, and I'm doing that now. You can use this one today, then I'll get permission from Billy and Agent Dees for the others. Stop being so difficult."

He was probably going to yell and scream at me again, but he took the high road and left the room. I settled in with my notes from this morning and began composing the story that would come from them.

Chapter 35

Even though Agent Dees had a thread or two of his own to weave into the drug landing storyline, I was not allowed in on the briefings because of the ongoing investigation into the drug pipeline. Agent Dees had taken particular delight in shutting the door in my face as he escorted Steve and me to the hall while he conferred with Billy. I should have followed Steve's lead and just walked out and left the building. Instead, I sat outside in the chairs reserved for those who are not in the inner circle. I tried not to pout. Grown women don't do it very well.

Afterward, when Agent Dees opened the door, he simply walked past me, not saying a word, leaving Billy to do the dirty work of telling me he could give me nothing more for the story, yet.

Steve, despite that, was quite happy with what he *had* been given from both Billy and Agent Dees. He felt like this front page rivaled our other one about Garth's murder and Senator Hughes's corruption charges, and he was sure he was going to be up for a journalist's award. I couldn't have cared less, having experienced the illusory "award for work well done" in the education business. It just wasn't worth it. Better to get a pizza and celebrate that way; it was a lot more certain.

"So, Mibbie, did Agent Dees say 'yes'?" Steve asked

idly as he was admiring his front page.

"No, he said I couldn't have it. The information is too tenuous and important to the case. Can you believe it? He actually walked right past me sitting in the hallway and didn't say a word. He made Billy do it."

"I'm not talking about information, I'm talking about the date."

"What date?"

"The date you asked him on when I gave you a day off and you decided to begin a romantic life again."

I knew it. I knew I would be sorry for making up a crummy lie.

"I chickened out."

"Really? 'Cause I thought you two looked awfully chummy over at Billy's office before I left."

"Oh please, he doesn't even like me. He made me leave when they were talking about the case. Billy never makes me leave. He just tells me what is on the record and what is off."

"Yeah, but that was business. How about before that?"

"You mean when we first walked in, and he got up to give you his chair, and not me?"

"That's right."

"Oh yes, I can see how you would think he was making a move on me. It just makes a girl's heart go pitty-pat when you are rude to her."

"He was teasing you. Can't you take a joke?"

"Yes, I can take a joke. What is it with you men trying to pass off your bad behavior as if it was something hilarious? It isn't."

"O, C'mon Mibbie. Give the guy a break. This is the first man who has even gotten your attention in years, much less given you his."

"I'll have you know I have had lots of male attention, especially lately."

"The car repair guy who fixed your window and the appliance repair technician who adjusted your dishwasher and fixed your stove do not count as male attention. You pay them to do what they do... Boy, that did not come out right at all."

"Forget it, Steve, I am not interested in Agent Dees, as the subject of a story or otherwise."

Even though Delago's murder had taken place two weeks ago, we resurrected the story to tie up the loose ends with Garth's murder. I felt bad for Garth. I, too, had gotten in over my head; I should be dead except for the goodness of others.

Garth's mother was bereft. It was so sad to see her in the midst of grief and the other journalists reveling in her shame, circling her like sharks in the bloody water. She'd been an icon in Morton society, living her life like it was a place in the sun, enjoying all of the requisite rewards of her son's notoriety and her husband's expansive influence. Now she had to live with the knowledge that not only was her son gone, but he was not gone heroically. He was linked to crime and violence.

"Boy, talk about a fall from grace," Steve said as he mused over the story tying Garth to Delago's murder.

"You know what they say: 'The bigger they are, the

farther they fall'."

"Yeah, and with Garth, power corrupted and absolute power got him killed."

"I feel sorry for his mom though; it's awful to lose a child any way it happens."

It didn't take long for Billy's boys to piece together the whole picture. I liked to think my fact gathering session with Harvey helped some. Senator Hughes was going to be indicted for conspiracy charges related to trying to move Garth into his Senate seat.

Garth had facilitated the drug traffic in our county with his mayoral influence and more state influence would have come as a consequence of Hughes's senatorial seat. Garth was going to repay the Senator with drug money. Whether or not the Senator knew that, was still under investigation, but Garth had entangled him enough that his career was wrecked. The Senator would also be answering financial disclosure questions related to the huge extra income he forgot to notify the IRS about.

Harvey had his own issues, and was quick to make a deal with anyone who wanted one, provided he was granted protective custody. I wasn't sure if he really believed they could protect him from bad people who wanted to kill him, but Harvey seemed like a relatively small fish when it came to the troubled waters of our little town, Morton.

The Senator was a much bigger one. He was willing to allocute to bribery charges, in addition to other felonious acts, but he stopped short of admitting to his contact with the drugs. He knew if Garth had been summarily dispatched, their new-found enemies would track him down in record time, too. He wasn't entirely sure he wasn't on their hit list anyway. Even though it had been Garth who had murdered Delago, not the Senator, he couldn't be sure they wouldn't draw the natural conclusion he had been a part of it and seek retribution, which was a gang standard.

It was clear now that Delago Fuentez had been on my interstate to meet what he thought was his local contact for the drug trade. Instead he had met Garth Miller's gun. Garth, in his zeal of self-confidence, had killed Delago, an MS-13 gang drug courier, thinking all the while that he, himself, could play the part of local drug lord. He had never had any dealings with MS-13, so he had no idea what he was up against.

Retribution came swiftly, in the form of a message to others not to do the same thing. They had killed Garth and placed his body in the exact location where Delago had been killed, then cut out his tongue and carved their initials in him. When Mike, the coroner, had looked closer, he could see they had cut a tear drop into the corner of Garth's eye, a gang sign that you have killed someone.

As a member of the gang, the teardrop would have been a tattoo, worn with pride. But Garth's had been carved in the corner of his eye as a deterrent to anyone thinking of killing a gang member. I shuddered to think he might have been alive while they did it.

Since Garth had controlled everything in our town for years, he had no reason to think the local law enforcement couldn't insulate him. They couldn't, especially not from so violent a gang as MS-13.

Garth had organized local drug activity through the gang at the Corn Dog. When the planes flew in the drugs, couriers on four wheelers loaded them into the waiting Hughes's Trucking Agency trucks. Garth's trucks hauled the drugs out to the big cities nearby, with some being kept by the local thugs to sell or redistribute.

Sadly, lots of the local drug traffic went to our college, while the rest of it hung around town, filtering into the high school. That was where Amber Tilton had gotten mixed up in it. It was the local gang, making a drop down that dirt road that led Fred to trouble and his ultimate retirement. They had behaved so boldly since they had inside information about the local law enforcement from Garth. Their presence near the college was now explained.

Once I gave over about Amber Tilton, Billy's investigators were quick to catch up with her. The Tiltons were shocked to find out what their daughter had been involved in. Most parents are. They made her cooperate to the best of her ability. Her "boyfriend" was rounded up and surprise, surprise, he was one of the jerks that had tried to push my car over the ravine at The Corn Dog.

That left only one mystery to be solved, and I was pretty sure I knew how to solve it without getting myself into trouble, probably a first for me.

Chapter 36

The house where Bretta's host family lived was situated in a lovely, well-kept neighborhood. I didn't think real people lived there, as there were no signs of life. The lawns were perfectly manicured. The flowers must have been replaced seasonally to give the illusion that there was constant blooming going on. No one was pruning, using a lawn mower, or sweeping away grass cuttings. No kids were riding their bikes. There wasn't even a mailman doing his route. It looked like a deadly gas attack had rendered the neighborhood empty.

Fortunately, the houses were clearly marked and the neighborhood easy to navigate, unlike many of the cookie-cutter housing projects that were in a labyrinth fit for a Greek mythological journey. I found number 4822 from the bold brass numbers on the mailbox post. I parked and walked up the sidewalk gingerly, afraid I might leave scuff marks in this immaculate place for which I expected there was a robotic policeman that would rush out to ticket me. I rang the doorbell and the chimes sounded out the beginning of Beethoven's 5th. It was the most pretentious doorbell I had ever heard.

Bretta answered the door. She had the baby on her hip and the three-year-old holding on to her leg. In the background, the other kids were running around the room, screaming and yelling. She looked even worse than when I had seen her at school last week. She just stood there.

"Bretta?" I said.

"Yes?"

"Bretta, it's me. Mibbie Wright. Do you remember me?"

"Yes, I talked to you when I came here. I saw you at the high school."

One of the boys ran up and kicked Bretta in the calf of her leg. She nearly dropped to the floor.

"Hey, you! Stop that!" I yelled. I never could abide bratty behavior.

"You can't tell me what to do. You're not my mother."

"I doubt your mother even tells you what to do, which is why you are behaving the way you are. Go get your mother, I want to talk to her."

"She's not here!" he yelled back at me as he ran like a terror through the living room. It was the kind of room you buy pre-decorated. You go in, pick it out, and the whole thing is delivered, right down to the fake flowers in the vases on the side tables.

"Where is she, Bretta?" I asked.

"Mr. and Mrs. Vinson have gone to the Bahamas for the week. I am taking care of the children."

"How long have they been gone?"

"This time for one week."

This time? I repeated in my head.

"This time," I said out loud. "Bretta, how many times since you have been here have they gone on a vacation?"

"Um, let me see, Colorado, Las Vegas, Cancun, New York…"

"Okay, that's enough. When was the last time you had a decent night's sleep?"

"I don't know. I can't remember."

Not surprisingly, since sleep deprivation causes memory loss.

"You go get some sleep. I'll take care of the kids."

Her protests were ineffectual. I think she wanted sleep more than anything in the world.

"Bretta, is this why you have been missing so much school?"

"Someone had to stay with the kids."

I took the baby out of her arms and detached the three-year-old from her leg. She staggered over to the couch in the living room and collapsed.

"Where is the stroller?" I asked the older brother.

"You can't go outside with her," he said.

"Why not?"

"She doesn't have her sippy cup."

"Well, suppose you get it for her. Fill it up with water and we'll take her for a walk!"

"Yea!" the older brother yelled. Didn't they ever get to go outside?

It was one of those perfect spring days. The sun was shining; the sky was blue; there were flowers in bloom everywhere, even though I suspected they were fake, too, like everything else here. No flowers ever looked that good. This place was all about facades. I took the kids for a walk around their neighborhood, then ventured down the way to a nearby park.

"We've never been here before," Mr. Loudmouth said. I was surprised, but the kids had so much fun racing around the enclosed area, sliding down the slide and pushing the merry-go-round that I could believe what he said. I found a baby swing and strapped the baby in. She was content and happy. I monitored the other kid's play to make sure they stayed busy *not* picking on each other.

After an hour of wild play, they settled down to a quiet dig in the sandbox. The baby had practically fallen asleep. When the three-year-old came over rubbing his eyes, I knew I would probably get a nap out of the two of them, at least. By laying down the inside of the baby stroller, I could fit the three-year-old in the front and the baby in the back. We'd make an easier trek home that way.

I made a game out of who could be the quietest when we came in the back door. We crept up the backstairs in the kitchen to the bedrooms, and I snuggled the baby down in her crib. The three-year-old had the rosy cheek of a healthy cherub. He lay down and immediately closed his eyes. His brothers were another story. Storybook or board game? Both would be quiet enough to let Bretta sleep, but it would require me to resurrect early parental abilities I hadn't tapped into in a while.

I don't think kids change too much even as the things in our lives get more modern. Children just want to know they matter, and giving them time shows them that. I settled on the board game; it looked brand new. I learned with my own children that if the rules of a game are too complicated they will rapidly lose interest in it, so since I didn't know the rules of this game, I decided to make them up. Reading the directions would require time I needed to keep the boys occupied.

"If you roll a double one, you get to move ten spaces. If you roll the dice off the board, you lose a turn. Otherwise, you have to add all the dots up on the dice and then move your man up and over."

I felt this was sufficiently difficult to hold their attention and easy enough to keep them playing. Of course, I had to play, too.

Somewhere along the line my stomach began to growl, and I realized we were all going to need to eat. Since I had graduated from cooking dinner for a young brood some years ago, and I had been a lousy representative lately for Good Mothers of America who feed their children healthy things in a timely manner, I had to really think about how to go about it. I reminded myself to kiss my girls when I got home tonight; I promised never to take them for granted.

Mama's injunction for a well-balanced dinner rang in my mind: "Start with the meat and build your starch and vegetables around it."

"Let's go make dinner," I announced.

"No," the boys whined in unison. They were sounding more and more like what I remembered their mother sounding like. Her whiney voice had been a precursor to the disreputable things I knew about her now. Note to self: villains often indicate their bad behavior in their voice tenor.

"We want to play," the boys yowled.

"Okay, then you play. I'll go and make dinner." I wondered if the sound of pots and pans was going to disturb Bretta. After sorting through the pizza rolls and the frozen chicken wraps, I decided these kids had not seen a decent meal since the dawn of time.

I needed help.

****

Elizabeth answered the house phone on the third ring. "Mom?"

"Bring the troops. I need help."

"Mom, did you say 'I need help'?"

"Yes, I said it; *I said it*."

She held the phone away from her ear. "Emily, Mom said she needed help."

I heard the phone switching hands. "Mom?"

"Yes, Emily."

"This is my mom, right?"

"Alright, let's not make a federal case out of this. I need help."

"Where are you?"

Never mind that when I said to bring the troops, I was only referring to my two daughters. My dad, a military man, practically raised me as a single-handed army myself. When he said "troops" he really only meant my sister and me. After she married and high-tailed it off to one of the "I" states, it was just me, but that didn't keep Daddy from referring to our joint efforts as troop maneuvers. It infuriated my sister that I could never remember if she lived in Idaho, Illinois or Iowa,

228

but they all started with an "I", and they were in the middle of the country, that much I knew. And that was about all I knew of her.

My "troops" showed up with food and supplies. Bretta was still asleep on the couch. I checked her to make sure she was still breathing. Child care was a lot easier with three instead of one. Emily loved the baby and the three-year-old thought she was there just for him. Elizabeth, a natural for the older boys, took them to the basement for a lively game of dodgeball. When it was time for bed, they were ready. No arguments, no excuses. Pajamas and bed.

I kissed my girls goodnight. I thought given poor Bretta's condition, it was best for me to stick around. I curled up on the couch in the den. Like an omen of my good behavior, *Big Jake* was the movie on TBS.

I awoke the next morning to the wailing of a baby. This must have been how the dawn greeted Bretta each day. I remembered enough about tending babies not to show up crib side without a bottle in hand. Sure enough, one spout quieted the other. One baby plus one bottle equaled silence.

Breakfast better be forthcoming or I was going to have banshee howling all over the house. The contents of the pantry were as dismal as the refrigerator and freezer. No cereal, oatmeal, grits or pancake makings. I don't know how the Vinson's expected Bretta to feed the kids with what was in the house. They apparently didn't care, because they had left no provisions or anything else. Even if she had money, which I doubted, Bretta had no car to drive to get her to the store. Just as I was contemplating the possibility of being seen in public in the same clothes that I had on yesterday, no shower and no toothbrush, there was a knock at the back door.

"We thought you could use some help, but we didn't think you would ask a second time."

My girls had brought breakfast!

What incredible kids I have! Bretta emerged from the living room. She had slept round the clock. Time for some phone calls to put a stop to this insanity.

Chapter 37

Call #1 The Vinsons
   Call #2 The Exchange Student Program director
   Call #3 Principal at the high school
   Call #4 Police
   Call #5 Child Welfare

One thing I missed about teaching was that sense of completion at the end of the year. For better or worse, it was all over, and there was closure. I also loved the first real week of summer vacation, which did not officially begin until at least two weeks after school had ended. That was because the first week of vacation was spent frantically completing things that had been left undone until "the end of school," and then recovering from the sheer exhaustion of it all. I had plenty of "sleeping around the clock" days myself just as Bretta had needed.

After finally getting enough rest, the fun began.

For me, it meant starting on my "Do-it-yourself" list of home improvement projects. It also meant some creative time. Sometimes that took the form of cooking a real meal, a true delight to the children after a month or two of being convinced they could bring me up on child abuse charges for some of the things they had had to eat for dinner while I was in the throws of "closing down school."

Life in the newspaper business was anything *but* this

example of a job with closure. If anything, one good week meant trying to top it the next week. There was no final, no ending, no finishing.

Spring was giving way to summer. I could feel it because it was time to put away my warm slippers and heavy robe. I was drinking my coffee on the front porch, feeling the gentle motion of the swing, one of the many things that make life so enjoyable, that I forget to do. This brief respite of morning coffee in my swing was the first quiet moment I had had in weeks, excluding the day off Steve had given me, and it seemed it would be the last one for a long time to come.

Things were changing in my own little world, but in the larger world of our little town, too. I had the impression of being tied to a runaway horse, all speed and no direction.

School was ending, and Elizabeth's graduation was tonight. We had bought the graduation dress and made reservations at a fancy restaurant in the big city nearby. This cause for celebration was momentous, and even the best that Morton could offer in cuisine was not good enough. My son was finishing up his finals and would streak in the driveway just in time for a quick shower and change. We'd unload the U-Haul that had his college things packed inside, tomorrow.

Bretta would be on a plane back to Norway in the morning. I was so glad to find out that what was wrong with her could be easily fixed with some rest and relaxation. If only all problems in life were that easy to solve. We had brought her home with us once the Vinsons had been summoned back from the Bahamas.

Their child care worries would be their own now, and I

doubted they would have enough in their bank account to pay someone to compensate for what Bretta was having to do for free. She'd managed to salvage something of her U. S. education, though she had told me confidentially that Norwegian education was a lot harder than American education.

Even though things were returning to "normal" they really weren't. At the end of this summer, another of my little chicks would be leaving the nest. Elizabeth had selected a college in another part of the state. I was grateful for college, the way it lets you get accustomed to your children being gone without them really being gone. College issues you into the inevitable change, that your children have grown up and moved on to their own lives, but keeps them coming home for long holidays and summer vacation, so the sever from you is not so complete.

Tonight we would all be together. Soon summer jobs and activities would order our lives, but tonight, we'd celebrate another happy event in our family with a long leisurely dinner where we'd laugh and talk and have time for each other. Like all golden moments it would be short-lived.

"Ready?" my daughter Elizabeth asked as she peeked into my bedroom just one hour before graduation. "I'm leaving now. We have to meet in the gym to get on our caps and gowns and get lined up in alphabetical order."

"Just about. Let me have a look at you."

She stepped in and swirled in her new dress to give me the full picture. I tried not to get weepy. I was going to do plenty of that at the ceremony.

"I want to give you your present now," I said as I pulled out the satin-lined blue box that I had kept hidden for almost a month.

"Now?" she asked eagerly. She untied the white satin ribbon that bound the box, then opened it up. "Oh mom, they are beautiful!"

"Every grown-up girl needs a string of pearls."

She held up her hair as I attached the safety catch and let them slide down her neck. I put my arms around her and squeezed as we both looked in the mirror at the lovely young woman this little girl had become.

"Hey, what are you two doing? Come on, we're going to be late." The voice of reason -the male in our family.

"You look pretty," John said to his sister. "Kiss her goodbye, mom, she has to get there early," he said to me.

Elizabeth left a peck on my cheek as she and her brother rushed off. Emily joined me for last minute hair and make-up touch-ups.

"Bretta, ready?" we called simultaneously, then piled into the car to drive to the high school. Already, cars were filling the parking lot, each family eager to get a front row view of their graduate. I wasn't worried. Press privileges have their place; I'd be getting a close-up of the Valedictorian and Salutatorian for the paper, so Steve had arranged for us to be seated directly in front of the podium. If he'd been a really nice boss, he wouldn't have made me work at all, but since I was going anyway, I didn't really mind.

"Pomp and Circumstance" started the water works for

me and probably every other mom in the building. A flurry of blue robes marched down the aisle. It was a good thing they were in order by name, because I was blinded by tears to tell which cap and gown belonged to my child. Having been an educator, I know that, even more than a wedding, it is a high school graduation that is filled with hope and possibility.

Of all of my graduations, (there were three) the high school one was the most meaningful, even though it was not the most financially profitable. A high school graduate does not earn as much with his or her diploma as a college one does. Yet, it is in this moment, on the cusp of adulthood, that graduation captures all of a young person's ambitions and dreams. All of "it," that great undefined "success," is still possible. A great task has been accomplished and new ones wait to be conquered.

Just in case there was still a dry eye in the house, the yearbook staff had put together a power-point presentation of the year's events. There were volleyball and football games, Homecoming courts and floats, Christmas pageants, basketball shots, Senior Picnic pictures, Prom, baseball, softball and soccer team pictures. There were candid shots and senior portraits, all memories of a year that had flitted by without anyone realizing it.

The speeches were good. I liked that the principal of the high school had the students write their own speeches. The top scholars of the senior class surely have the words of wisdom needed to share with their peers. I learned early on as a teacher that students listen to each other far better than they listen to the adult in the room.

I snapped the Valedictorian and Salutatorian pictures as unobtrusively as possible. It was difficult enough to be that young and to have to master your nerves, addressing so many people. I didn't need to make it harder for them by snapping pictures in their faces and throwing them off with my flashes.

And just like every other magical moment in our lives, this one was over in a heartbeat. The kids always try to hang onto it by lingering for goodbyes, but nothing can stop the march of time. I gathered up my brood for the trip into the big city. I'd be up early tomorrow morning to get Bretta off to the airport, so I wanted to get started on our late night.

Traffic from our interstate flushed me into the harrowing city streets of our neighboring big city in no time. We found a park miraculously within two blocks of Restaurante Escorial, a restaurant that specialized in Spanish cuisine. In honor of taking Spanish I and II, Elizabeth wanted to order all our meals in the authentic language. The girls were all wearing at least three inch tiny heels, but they laughed at my suggestion that they take them off for the walk to the restaurant. They staggered in, and the maitre d' took us to our table.

We had *paella,* cooked over an open fire, made with lobster head stock (the most flavorful part of a lobster to the tongue, if the most unappetizing in thought) and chanterelle mushrooms in *salmora.* We watched as the chef cooked it, then placed it in the center of the table for us all to eat family-style. We dipped our spoons in and ate from the large pan together. It was a wonderful, communal way to eat our meal, and the perfect ending to a significant family event.

I took pictures in my mind of these scenes: Elizabeth's beaming face, Emily's smile as she gave Elizabeth her graduation gift, of Bretta watching our family interact, my son as he played the role of squiring four women around all night. Some images don't require film. Very tired, but very happy, we walked back to the car at 11:30, and made our way home. Once we returned, the house was silent in no time.

Next morning, I helped Bretta stack her suitcases in the trunk. The kids all came out to tell her goodbye with promises of Facebook contacts and texting messages. We hurried off to get her through security, which would take longer, since it was an international flight.

When I got home, the girls had already started helping their brother unload the U-Haul trailer. I was grateful, and between the four of us, we stored all of his things in the basement and in his room. I helped Elizabeth pack for her senior trip to the beach with her friends before their summer jobs started the following Monday, then made a huge sub sandwich for us all to eat.

Chapter 38

Steve had been kind about letting me off early, so I could get ready for the graduation, and about letting me come in late, so I could get Bretta off to the airport, but his contentedness soon gave way to his ambition. We had set records for paper sales, which have been down with the advent of on-line reading. He was ecstatic to see the numbers when our stories broke about little Morton's acquaintance with drugs and gang activity. Like every good newspaper man, he craved more. Short of killing someone important myself, I wasn't sure how that was going to happen.

I had started with a story on the new police chief. While the old one had disappeared, the FBI would inevitably track him down. That would be a whole other story line. The new police chief was hired from the outside, because the city council realized how it looked to have had both the head city administrator and city law enforcement officer involved in such a scandal. Of course, there are small towns that continue in their politically corrupt ways even though they have been found out, but I liked to think our little town had more pride than that.

Our new city police chief was not only from another state, he was from another region. He had already butted heads with some of our city leaders over things that seemed inconsequential to those outside the South: manners. Still, all regionally preferred behavior aside, I felt this man would be a good needle on our moral compass gone awry. He and Billy got along well, and as far as I was concerned, that stood him in good stead. Billy would not have liked him if he had sensed any impropriety in him.

I pulled into my parking place and gathered my purse up off the front seat where I had idly tossed it, feeling uninspired about being at work. Gladys handed me a few message slips to decipher on my way back to my desk, her illegible handwriting somehow comforting. Some things never change. I got out my camera to retrieve the pictures from the graduation, and began work on the story, "Graduates Head Out into the World."

"Got a call from your sheriff this morning," Steve said as he leaned around the corner of our office's makeshift kitchen.

"Oh yeah, what did he say?"

"Says he and Mr. Henderson, the new police chief, have some information to share with you. Can you get over there?"

"Sure, I'll get right over, just as soon as I've finished this story on graduation."

"Nope, go now."

"But Steve...."

"Go!"

I was puzzled why he was in such a big hurry to get me over there. After all, this story had to be written, but I picked up my notebook and camera and shuttled out the back door to go over to Billy's office.

"Whaddya want?" Bruce Tyner growled from behind the front desk. I was certainly back at work, now.

"I have a meeting with Sheriff Bartlett and Mr. Henderson."

"Who says?"

"Sheriff Bartlett."

"Nobody told me nothin'."

Should I say it? Should I say, "That doesn't surprise me in the least"? No, be nice, be nice.

"Really? Well, why don't you buzz back and ask the Sheriff. I'm sure he'll tell you to send me right back."

"No."

"No, what?"

"No, I ain't gonna buzz him."

I was exasperated. This was carrying a personal grudge too far.

"Alright then, I will simply issue myself into his presence, since I have been *invited*, and there is no reason not to think I am not expected, despite your feeling otherwise." In other words, watch it buddy, I have now hauled out the proper grammar!

Bruce gave me that look my students used to give me of "What did she just say?" and I tossed my head up into the air with a hint of the effrontery I felt and proceeded down the hall to Billy's office, ready to use my pen as a weapon in case Bruce tried to stop me. When I went into Billy's office, I was feeling triumphant.

Billy smiled and said, "Okay, what is it? You look like

240

the cat that got the cream."

"I just told *that* Bruce Tyner off. He would not buzz back here to tell you that I was here, so I told him, I would just come back here anyway, and he could try to stop me."

"He doesn't know how."

"I know. No one knows how to stop me. I feel I could conquer the world." I was now ebullient. No one could stop me!

"I've tried and tried to get him to learn how to buzz people from the front office and to transfer phone calls, but he just won't do it."

"Oh. He doesn't know how to *buzz*." My delusions of grandeur as always, were short-lived.

"Yeah. That's what I said. He doesn't know how to buzz back here. What did you think I meant?"

I was sure I reddened. Was my deflating ego as evident as the air escaping from a balloon? I slid a side glance at Mr. Henderson and saw him smiling. Great. All I needed was for him to have a laugh at my expense. Billy tried not to look up, aware that I had just embarrassed myself.

"Mibbie, in case you haven't met him yet, this is Mr. Tom Henderson, our new city police chief. We've been going over some ideas for getting the municipal law enforcement back on track, and we thought a good way to inform the public was through *The World*. We want people to feel safe and assured that our new police chief will be straightening things out and both the city and the county law enforcement are working together. Mr. Henderson is doing a great job."

I shook hands with the new police chief and pulled out my pad.

"What exactly would you like to say?"

"We'd like to start with showing the city police force in a more transparent light. Let's make it clear that the past is the past and we are moving on with a new administration. I didn't think it would be a good idea to clean house immediately, but clearly some of the personnel will have to go," Mr. Henderson began.

"Do you want that made public?" I asked, knowing that we were treading on personal rights law here.

"I think it's best if we leave the personnel changes to the city council actions at the next meeting. We'll call a private session because we are discussing the good name and character of someone, then you can report that several, or however many we let go, personnel changes have taken place." Chief Henderson sat forward as he talked, a sign we were being confidential.

"I agree. That's a good course of action. It will just stir up people to know who has lost his or her job."

"The city council will be acting on your recommendations only; it will muddy the waters as to who is actually responsible," put in Billy.

Poor Billy, he had his fair share of angry phone calls and hateful comments from the townspeople when he had had to do the same thing, only there was no one to spare him. The county commission hadn't helped at all.

"How do you want your office to be viewed?" I asked the chief.

"As a place to solve problems," he responded. I thought Mr. Henderson had a good answer.

"What are your projected goals?"

"I want to address the drug issue right away. Next, I want to address the issue of the gang activity that has crept in, and I want to get rid of this renegade group of kids we have around here. Will I be offending too many people with that comment?"

Billy had obviously prepped the chief as to why he would bring me in. Good leaders can use the press to bring about good change. Those in the journalism business who faulted Billy and my relationship were those who saw public servants and the press as adversaries. I could understand that with someone who was corrupt like Garth or Senator Hughes, but Billy was as honest and hard working as anyone would want. To make my world and that of the people in this community better, we needed to work together.

"I think you might offend only those parents who have let their kids run riot, and not disciplined them themselves. The citizens of this city who have been upset by them will be grateful," I responded, aware that as a past educator and current parent, I would be one of the people who would be appreciative.

We talked a little while longer and then I reviewed with both of them the story line I had in mind. We agreed it would make a great second page story. No need to shove changes in the public face. Besides, I was sure Steve was going to claim the front page for more exciting stories. I headed back to the office.

"So, what'd they give you?" Steve asked from the kitchen when I came back to my desk. By now I was suspicious. Why was he in the kitchen again, or had he even left? If that was true, was he on an eating binge?

I took the opportunity to hoist my purse onto my desk and go into the kitchen myself.

"It's a story about the new police chief's clean-up."

"That's all?"

"Yeah, what did you think it was?"

"I was hoping they'd found that police chief and they were bringing him in."

"Nope, just meeting the new police chief."

"So, what do you think?"

"I like him; more importantly, Billy likes him. You know, 'men know men; women know women.'"

"Don't let Gladys hear you say that. You just set the Women's Movement back about three hundred years. I think I hear some suffragettes turning over in their graves."

"Give me a break, Steve. You know what I mean. A man can fool a woman every time, but he can't fool another man."

"So, you're saying women don't know how to read men?"

"No! I'm saying that when it comes to men, women aren't as clear about them as another man would be. It isn't sexist, it's just admitting the truth. Besides, it isn't sexist for me to say that men can be manipulative. It would be sexist for me to say that women are not smart enough to figure it out."

"Just don't try your logic out on anybody who doesn't

know you. So, what story are you doing."

"An intro piece on Mr. Henderson, I told you."

"That's it?"

"Yes, what more do you want?"

I looked around to see if he was hiding something.

"What more do I want? You can ask that after I've had murder and mayhem and mischief on my front page?"

"I'd like to remind you that I've had frantic fear and fountains of fury and foul play on *my* front page! Did you think of that?"

"C'mon Mibbie, be a sport. Let's get a really good front page this week. And I don't think the new police chief angle is going to do it."

"Look, Steve …" I started to say. Then I stopped. There in front of me was a calendar and I realized it was almost June.

"You know what? You are absolutely right. You need a really good front page. And you need to figure out what that is going to be. I am exhausted. I have been your front page for about two months now and I just realized that my time has come. I've got a date with a beach chair, an umbrella and a book."

What I needed was a vacation. And I was going to take it! I turned to Steve and said, "It's 10:30. You have precisely seven more hours out of me, then I am going to go home. Tomorrow I'm going to make reservations for the beach house and my children and I are going to the beach for our usual week of vacation. Whatever week that happens to be, I'm taking it, even if it means next week. So get ready, Steve, you're going to have to live without me for a while. Now I'll bet those suffragettes of yours are jumping up and down to congratulate me for telling a male boss off."

I thought he'd get really mad. Instead, he looked sheepishly towards the refrigerator. He opened the door and pulled out a cake that read: "Congratulations Mibbie: Best Reporter Ever!"

Of course I felt crummy. That was going to be the icing on the big slice of guilt I was having for being so selfish.

"You're right, of course," Steve said. "You have been through a lot, and you do need a break. I'm sorry for not seeing it. Here, have a piece of cake. Go ahead and call about your beach house and see when they can get you in."

I was just scraping my heart off the floor where it had fallen into a million pieces for being so awful when I caught sight of a memo from the head office commending Steve for his news coverage of the recent troubles in Morton. And the only thing he was going to share with me was a store bought cake.

Suddenly, the gloves came off.

I turned and went to my desk. I pulled my phone out of my purse and smashed in the numbers to the beach house landlady with a force that could have punched them through the cell phone cover.

Beachside, here I come!

Made in the USA
Columbia, SC
03 January 2026